Raves For the Work of of MAX ALLAN COLLINS!

"Crime fiction aficionados are in for a treat...a neo-pulp noir classic."
— *Chicago Tribune*

"No one can twist you through a maze with as much intensity and suspense as Max Allan Collins."
— *Clive Cussler*

"Collins never misses a beat...All the stand-up pleasures of dime-store pulp with a beguiling level of complexity."
— *Booklist*

"Collins has an outwardly artless style that conceals a great deal of art."
— *New York Times Book Review*

"Max Allan Collins is the closest thing we have to a 21st century Mickey Spillane and...will please any fan of old-school, hardboiled crime fiction."
— *This Week*

"Few people alive today can tell a story better than Max Allan Collins."
— *Book Reporter*

"This book is about as perfect a page turner as you'll find."
— *Library Journal*

"Bristling with suspense and sexuality, this book is a welcome addition to the Hard Case Crime library."
— *Publishers Weekly*

What kind of makeup, I thought, requires a girl taking off her panties?

She was naked as she walked over to the shelves with the sound system and picked out a homemade cassette tape and inserted it into the machine. "Smoke on the Water" by Deep Purple burst out of the speakers like the thunder had returned.

Then she cranked it some more.

She asked, almost shouting, "Could you switch off the bed-side lamp?"

I said I could, and did.

"Can you watch me from there?" she yelled sweetly. "Does it hurt? I'm gonna work it over here."

I swung my body around, ribs complaining just a little, but the hell with them. Though darkness had returned, I could tell she was moving the coffee table to one side and making a little performance area out of the throw rug.

Then she went over to a nearby wall switch and a click announced overhead black-light tubing coming on to make Jimi and the Fudge and Janis glow. Also her lips and her finger- and toenails and the tips of her breasts and the petals of flesh between her legs—all glowing red as she did a swaying dance to the thumping music, arms waving, feet shifting weight from leg to leg, the mirrored wall behind me echoing and multiplying her. Then she began to twist and grind in rhythm with the pounding guitar riff, a native dance that grew in intensity, lifting right fist and left knee, then left fist and right knee, swinging her arms, her torso, awkward, graceful, until finally she tossed herself on the couch on her back and spread her legs, summoning me...

The Wrong
QUARRY

by **Max Allan Collins**

A HARD CASE CRIME NOVEL

A HARD CASE CRIME BOOK
(HCC-114)
First Hard Case Crime edition: January 2014

Published by

Titan Books
A division of Titan Publishing Group Ltd
144 Southwark Street
London SE1 0UP

in collaboration with Winterfall LLC

Print Edition ISBN 978-1-78116-266-8
E-book ISBN 978-1-78116-267-5

Design direction by Max Phillips
www.maxphillips.net

Typeset by Swordsmith Productions

The name "Hard Case Crime" and the Hard Case Crime logo are trademarks of Winterfall LLC. Hard Case Crime books are selected and edited by Charles Ardai.

Printed in the United States of America

Visit us on the web at www.HardCaseCrime.com

For John Mull
who likes 'em down and dirty

THE WRONG QUARRY

*"It's frightening how easy it is
to commit murder in America."*
W. H. AUDEN

*"Someone once told me that
every minute, a murder occurs.
So I don't want to waste your time.
I know you want to go back to work."*
ALFRED HITCHCOCK

ONE

For a guy who killed people for a living, he was just about the most boring bastard I ever saw.

I had been tailing him for two days, as he made his way from Woodstock, Illinois, where he owned an antiques shop on the quaint town square, to…well, I didn't know where yet.

So far it had been every little town—on a circuitous route taking us finally to Highway 218—with an antiques shop, where he would go in and poke around and come out with a few finds to stow in the trunk of his shit-brown Pontiac Bonneville.

If it hadn't been for the explosion of red hair with matching beard that made his head seem bigger than it was, he would have been a human bowling pin, five-foot-eight of flab in a gray quilted ski jacket. He wore big-frame orange-lensed glasses both indoors and out, his nose a potato with nostrils and zits, his lips thick and purple. That this creature sometimes sat surveillance himself seemed like a joke.

I was fairly certain he was on his way to kill somebody—possibly somebody in Iowa, because that was the state we'd been cutting down on the vertical line of Highway 218. Right now we were running out of Iowa and the flat dreary landscape was threatening to turn into Missouri.

Soon there would be fireworks stands—even though it was crisp November and the Fourth of the July a moot point—and people would suddenly speak in the lazy musical tones of the South, as if the invisible line on the map between these Midwestern states was the Mason–Dixon.

Some people find this accent charming. So do I, if it's a buxom wench with blonde pigtails getting out of her bandana blouse and cut-off jeans in a hayloft. Otherwise, you can have it.

Right now my guy was making a stop that looked like a problem. Turning off and driving into some little town to check out an antiques shop was manageable. No matter how small that town was, there was always somewhere I could park inconspicuously and keep an eye on Mateski (which was his name—Mateski, Ronald Mateski…not exactly Bond, James Bond).

But when he pulled off and then into the gravel lot of an antiques mini-mall on the edge of a town, I had few options. Pulling into the lot myself wasn't one of them, unless I was prepared to get out and go browsing with Mateski.

Not that there was any chance he'd make me. I had stayed well back from him on the busy two-lane, and when he would stop to eat at a truck stop, I would either sit in my car in the parking lot, if that lot were crowded enough for me to blend in, or take a seat in the trucker's section away from the inevitable booth where Mateski had set down his big ass.

This time I had no choice but to go in and browse. Had there been a gas station and mini-mart across the way, I could have pulled in there. But this was a tin-shed antiques mall that sat near a cornfield like a twister had plopped it down.

Mateski's penchant was primitive art and furniture—apparently it was what sold well for him back in rustic Woodstock. He didn't have his truck with him (a tell that he wasn't *really* out on a buying trip), so any furniture would have to be prime enough to spend shipping on; but he did find a framed oil that he snatched up like he'd found a hundred-dollar bill on the pavement—depicting a winter sunset that looked like your half-blind grandmother painted it.

I stopped at stalls with used books and at one I picked up a few Louis L'Amour paperbacks I hadn't read yet, making sure I was still browsing when he left. Picking him up again would be no problem. He'd be getting back on Highway 218 and heading for somewhere, probably in Missouri. Hannibal maybe. Or St. Louis.

But when I got back on the road, I thought I'd lost him. Then I spotted his mud-spattered Bonneville at a Standard pump, said, "Fuck," and took the next out-of-sight illegal U-turn I could to go back.

When I got there, he was inside paying. I could use some gas myself, so I turned my dark green Ford Pinto over to the attendant and went into the restaurant side of the small truck stop and took a piss. Mateski was gone when I got out, which was fine. I paid for my gas, bought gum and a Coke, and hit the road again, picking him up soon, always keeping a couple cars between us.

This is just how exciting yesterday and today had been. Not the Steve McQueen chase in *Bullitt*. But despite his fat ass and his thing for lousy art, Mateski was a dangerous guy. That he usually worked the passive side of a two-man contract team didn't mean he hadn't killed his share himself. The Broker had always insisted that the passive side of a duo had to take the active role once out of every four jobs. Keep your hand in. Use it or lose it.

The Broker had been the middleman through whom I used to get my assignments. I much preferred the active role, coming in for a day or two and handling the wet work, rather than sitting for a couple of weeks in cars and at surveillance posts taking detailed notes as to habits and patterns of a target.

Don't get me wrong. I don't enjoy killing. I just don't mind. It's something I learned to do overseas, as a sniper, where I developed the kind of dispassionate attitude needed for that kind of work. Killing is a necessary evil, as they say, although I don't know that it's all that evil in a lot of cases. War and self-defense, for instance.

On the other hand, there was one notorious asshole in the trade who specialized in torture. I mention him in passing now, but eventually it will have some importance. File it away.

As for me, my name is unimportant, but when I first started killing people for money—not counting Vietnam—I worked through the Broker. This tall, slender, dapper, distinguished-looking man of business, who might have been a banker or a CEO, recruited people like me, who had unwittingly learned a trade in the employ of Uncle Sam. He was something of a pompous ass—for example, he called me Quarry, which was a sort of horseshit code name, derived from my supposed cold-ness ("Hollow like carved-out rock," he said once) and also ironic, since the targets were *my* quarry.

So Broker's people that I worked with called me "Quarry" and I got used to it. On occasion I even used it as the last name of a cover identity, and as it happens, this was one of those occasions. John R. Quarry, according to my Wyoming driver's license, Social Security and Mastercard. So for our purpose here, that name will do as well as any.

I should probably clue you in a little about me. I was closer to thirty than forty, five ten, one hundred-sixty-five pounds, short brown hair, but not military short. Kept in shape, mostly through swimming. Handsome enough, I suppose, in a bland, unremarkable way. When was this? Well, Reagan hadn't been president long enough for his senility to show (much), and everybody was hurting from the recession.

Well, actually, I wasn't. Hurting. I lived quietly, comfortably and alone in an A-frame cottage on Lake Paradise near Geneva,

Wisconsin. I had no one woman, but the resort area nearby meant I was rarely lonely. I had a small circle of friends who thought I sold veterinary medicine, but really I was semi-retired from the killing business.

"Semi" because I still kept my hand in, but not in the old way. After the Broker betrayed me and I got rid of him, I sort of inherited what today would be called a database, but back then was just a small pine file cabinet. Within it was what was essentially a list of over fifty names of guys like me, who had worked for the Broker—detailed info on each, photos, addresses, down to every job they'd gone on.

Since I was out of work, after killing the Broker, I'd had an intriguing idea. I could see how I could use the Broker's file, and keep going, in a new way, on my own terms. After destroying the information on myself, I would choose a name and travel to where that party lived and stake him or her out (a few females were on the list), then follow said party to their next job.

Through further surveillance, I would determine their target's identity, approach that target, and offer to eliminate the threat. For a healthy sum, I would discreetly remove the hit team. For a further fee, I might—depending on the circumstances—be able to look into who had hired the hit done, and remove that threat as well.

The risks were considerable. What if a target—approached with a wild story from a stranger claiming to be a sort of contract killer himself—called the authorities, or otherwise freaked out?

But I was well aware that anyone designated for death was somebody who had almost certainly done something worth dying over. Targets of hitmen tend not to be upstanding citizens, unless they are upstanding citizens with down-and-dirty secrets. And weren't they likely to be aware that they presented a problem to some powerful, merciless adversary? The kind of adversary who would be capable of such an extreme solution…?

From the start, I felt confident that such people would welcome my help. After all, their other option was to take a bullet
or get hit by a car or have one of those accidental long drops off
a short pier. And the fee I could charge—most people value
their *own* lives highly—would mean I'd only have to take on
these risky tasks perhaps a couple of times a year.

On the other hand, those "couple of times" required a huge
amount of spec work. First, I always chose from the Broker's
list names whose preference was passive, meaning I was guar-
anteeing myself a considerable amount of surveillance—but
this was necessary, because if I followed the active participant
to a kill, the passive half might already be in the wind, leaving a
dangerous loose end. Both halves needed removal.

I had been lucky a few times, and staked out parties who
within a few weeks had gone out on a job, minimizing my layout of time. But professionals in the killing game—again, because
of the risk and the high fees—seldom take more than three or
four jobs a year. At least the teams working for the Broker didn't.

That meant I could sit stakeout—renting a house across from
a subject, for example, sitting in car like a damn cop drinking
coffee after coffee from paper cups—for literally months. This
had happened several times. So I had begun to take measures
to limit my expenditure of time.

Ronald Mateski was a good example.

Once I had determined Mateski was an antiques dealer, I
began to call his Woodstock shop once a week from a series of
pay phones in the Geneva area. If I got Mateski, I would ask for
the business hours, or mutter wrong number. If I got a clerk,
usually a female, I would say that I had an item I wanted to
bring into the shop for Mr. Mateski to appraise—would he be
around next week?

And when at last I'd been told Mr. Mateski would be gone for two weeks on a buying trip, going to estate auctions and the like, I thanked the girl, hung up, and smiled to myself…knowing that Mr. Mateski was heading out on a job.

And the length of time he'd be away meant that he was, as usual, taking the passive role.

That had meant a comparatively painless (if still painful) two days of tailing Ronald Boring Mateski to wherever the fuck he was heading—Iowa? Arkansas, God help me?—and determining his target: the person he would be gathering information on for the active half of the team, the killer who would be arriving at some indeterminate time in the near future.

Indeterminate because these killing teams—particularly now that the Broker was out of the picture—sometimes maintained surveillance for several weeks, and other times for as little as a few days.

My prep for this trip had been minimal. Select an I.D., pack clothes including a couple of nondescript sport coats and suits and white shirts and ties and the sweatshirts and polos and jeans I preferred, a few guns (my nine millimeter, a noise suppressor, and a back-up .38 snubnose revolver), a hunting knife in sheath, switchblade, lock picks, canister of chloroform, rags, several pairs of surgical gloves, some duct tape, a coil of clothesline. The usual.

And of course I'd driven a good distance from my home area to buy the 1980 Pinto, which cost a grand cash, the kind of nothing car that helps nobody notice you.

Around four o'clock, Mateski pulled off and drove twenty miles—longer than any previous antiques-buying detour—into Stockwell, Missouri, whose WELCOME TO sign included all the requisite lodges and an interesting designation: "Little Vacationland of Missouri."

We'd barely got past the city limits before he pulled into a row-of-cabins-style motel called the Rest Haven Court. It looked clean and well-maintained, and even had a small tarp-covered swimming pool. But it obviously dated back to Bonnie and Clyde days. Mateski stopped at the slightly larger cabin near the neon sign to check in.

Directly across the street was a modest-size Holiday Inn and that's where I pulled in, but for now I just sat in the lot, watching across the way in my rear-view mirror. Mateski must have had a reservation, because it took him under three minutes to register. Then he was back in the Bonneville to drive over to the farthest of twelve cabins, where he parked. Only three other cars were in the spaces at cabins. From his trunk, out from under the crap paintings he'd bought, he withdrew a small suitcase, and went over to the door marked 12 and let himself in.

I got out, stretched, yawned, making something of a show of it. Got my fleece-lined leather bomber jacket out of the back seat and slipped it on; I was otherwise in a sweatshirt, jeans and running shoes.

Was he in for the night?

Surely he would have to get settled. He might not even start surveillance till tomorrow. I decided to risk it.

At the desk, I asked for a second-floor room facing the street. The female clerk, a pleasant, permed platinum blonde in her twenties wearing big-frame glasses (much nicer than Mateski's and minus the rust-color lenses), informed me that I could have just about any room in the place.

"This is the start of off-season," she said chirpily. She had big brown eyes and a Judy Holliday voice—well, it was the Holiday Inn, wasn't it?

"An off-season for what?"

Very nice, very white smile. She might be worth cultivating as a source and, well…cultivating.

"Stockwell Park is the nicest fun spot this side of the Ozarks," she said. "People come from all over."

"Oh?"

She nodded and that mane of frizzy hair bounced. "Trails, trees, all kinds of greenery, so much space. Tennis courts, volleyball, playgrounds, swimming pool. Duck pond, too. Also, Stockwell Field is near there—we have a triple-A ball club, you know."

"In a town of twenty thousand?"

"Oh, Stockwell really hops in the summer. If we hadn't had this cold snap…and, uh, you know, the recession…we'd be doing land-office business, even now."

"Must get a little dull around here, then."

"It can be. We have live music in the lounge, on the weekend, if you're planning to stay that long."

This was Thursday.

"I might be here a week or more," I said. "Is there a reduced rate for that?"

"There is, if you pay a week in advance."

So we did the strictly business thing, and I got all checked in as John Quarry, but our eyes and mouths were being friendly. Maybe I could get laid on this trip. I already felt like I deserved it, after two days of Ronald Mateski. She seemed like a nice girl, and with her working here, so convenient.

I went up to the room, which I will not insult your intelligence by describing, and placed my suitcase on the stand, got my toiletries distributed on the counter in the john. Shower, no tub. The TV was a 21" Sony, which was nice, and they had a satellite dish, so I'd get a lot of stations. The double bed's mattress seemed a little soft, but I'd live. I went to the window, drew back the curtain, and *shit*, Mateski's car was gone.

I'd managed to fuck up already, making goo-goo eyes at the desk clerk. Someday maybe I would learn to think with the big head.

Not panicking, I took time to throw some water on my face, toweled off, brushed my teeth, decided on the luxury of taking a shit, during which I thought about my options.

Mateski was not here in an active capacity. He would undoubtedly watch the target for at least a week. Certainly nothing less than four days—the bare minimum to get patterns down. So I had no reason to lose my cool. I could wait till tomorrow and pick him up then, or I could drive around small-town Stockwell and see if I could spot his Bonneville. I decided on the latter.

It was a nice little city, well-off—the older homes well-maintained with big yards; numerous housing additions expanded the town's edges, with only one small trailer park to indicate anybody here would feel hard times. The downtown had a rustic look not unlike Mateski's Woodstock, but without a town square—four blocks of businesses faced each other across four lanes. Many businesses included the Stockwell name— STOCKWELL BANK AND TRUST, STOCKWELL INSURANCE, STOCKWELL TRAVEL, and so on. I spotted a large newish high school, tan brick with architecture that said late sixties, a smaller, older Catholic high school, a late fifties/early sixties grade school. A grand-looking county courthouse dated to the late 1800s, as did the similar city hall, just off the main drag.

The park area the desk clerk had extolled was on the west side of town, and I drove through it, winding around a vast expanse of green with the promised sports facilities, though at the far side there was an unexpectedly rocky and hilly area with a stream running through it. This section was mostly inaccessible by car.

This was the kind of all-American town President Reagan mistakenly thought was typical for the nation, the kind of near-fantasy that Norman Rockwell painted for the *Saturday Evening Post* and that the Jewish moguls at MGM cooked up for Andy Hardy and his Christian audience during the Depression.

Also on the west side was a hilly area of mostly older homes, perhaps not quite as well-maintained but nothing to give the city fathers fits. I cruised this neighborhood and that's when I spotted him.

He was, as is good surveillance practice, sitting in the back seat of the Bonneville. That was wise a couple of ways—people who saw Mateski would assume he was waiting for somebody, and those who glanced at the vehicle, seeing no one in front, particularly after dark (which it was), would not notice him at all.

He was almost directly across from a big black cement-block building that sat on the corner atop the hill with two terraced levels that cement stairs with railing climbed. Across the front of the building, above windows and doors, in very white bold letters, were the words VALE DANCE STUDIO. Lights were on in the building, glowing yellow like a jack-o'-lantern's eyes.

I drove around the block, which required going down the hill, and came up behind the building, where a cement drive taking a sharp turn to enter was labeled VALE DANCE STUDIO PARKING — PRIVATE. What the hell. I pulled in.

Maybe twenty-five cars were waiting there, most with motors running—an interesting mix that included a good share of high-end numbers, Lincolns and Caddies. Men and women, sometimes couples but mostly not, were sitting in the vehicles, a few standing in the cold, smoking.

I pulled the Pinto into a space and got out and walked over in the cold to a woman in a full-length mink coat; her oval face was pretty, with bright red lipstick and jeweled glasses. She was my age, maybe a little older. She was smoking, her hands in leather gloves.

"I'm lost," I lied, my breath making as much smoke as her cigarette. "Can you point me to the Holiday Inn?"

She gave me directions that I didn't need with a smile that I didn't mind. Then I made a move like I was heading back to my car, only to stop and give her my own smile, curiosity-tinged.

I asked, "What *is* this place?"

"Can't you read?" she said, blowing smoke, not bitchy, just teasing.

Big letters saying VALE DANCE STUDIO were across the back of the black cement-block building as well. It was an odd squat-looking building, like a hut got way out of hand, not quite two stories with all the windows fairly low-slung.

"I'm gonna take a wild swing and say it's a dance studio," I said, grinning, my breathing pluming, my hands tucked in the pockets of my fleece-lined jacket. Wouldn't she be surprised to know my right hand was gripping a nine millimeter Browning.

"Yeah," she said, breathing smoke, nodding, clearly chilly, "I used to go come here all the time as a kid."

"You're a dancer, huh?"

"Not really. It was a skating rink when I was in school. We came here all through elementary and junior high."

"Sure. All skate. Ladies' choice. The ol' mirrored disco ball, before they even called it that."

She smiled and laughed and it was smoky in a bunch of ways. "Skating's gone the way of the dodo bird, I guess."

"Except for roller derby."

"Ha!" She nodded toward the building. "It's a dance studio, as you've gathered. Students are junior high and high school girls."

"Oh, you're here to pick up your daughter?"

"Two of them. One I think has a real chance."

"Chance for what?"

"Mr. Roger is working with both my girls, the younger for Miss Teenage Missouri, the older for Miss Missouri. But it's my young one who has a real chance."

"Beauty pageants, huh?"

"They're mostly just called pageants now. You know." She shrugged shoulders thick with mink. "Times change."

"Sure do. They fired Bert Parks, didn't they? So, did you say Mr. Rogers? Like on TV?" I knew she hadn't, but I was milking it.

"No, Mr. *Roger*. Roger Vale. It's his studio. He is *so* gifted. And I don't care what anybody says. We stand behind him. Look at all these cars."

"What do you mean?"

She waved at the air and her cigarette made white trails. "You know how it is. People always talk. It's because he's different. That's all I'll say about the matter.....*Oh*, there's Julie and Bobbi!"

She dropped her cigarette, toed it out, and waved. Out the back of the building's two rear glass doors, teenage girls in fall and winter coats were emerging, chattering, smiling, laughing. They had a small flight of cement stairs to come down, about a third of what was in front of the building.

"Nice meeting you," I said to the mother, though neither of us had exchanged names.

"You, too," she said, and beamed.

Maybe I should have got her name. That desk clerk wasn't a lock, you know.

I got in the Pinto.

Soon I was heading through the intersection of this otherwise residential neighborhood and could see the brown Bonneville parked in the same place. A few daughters were coming down those front steps with parents picking them up on this side. But not many.

I drove on through and took a left down the other side of the hill, and came around the adjacent block to park on the opposite side of the street, down a ways but with a good view of the Bonneville, its engine off, just another parked vehicle. Me, too. I sat there in the cold, the Pinto's engine off too, wishing I'd grabbed something to eat, but unlike Mateski, I remained in the front seat. I wanted to be able to take off quickly, if need be.

Was he shadowing one of these wealthy parents?

That seemed a good bet. This was a money town, and these were money moms and dads, for the most part.

For whatever reason—maybe some parents had gone inside to have a word with the dance instructor—it was a good hour before the lights in the big black building went out. All the daughters, all the parents, were long gone by now. I started the car up, drove slowly past the parked Bonneville, and again went around the block, down the hill, and came up around and into the parking lot.

Only two cars remained on the gravel—a baby-blue Mustang and a red Corvette, parked very near the foot of the small slope behind the building. Not Lincolns or Caddies, but two very choice automobiles, it seemed to me, especially driving a fucking Pinto.

But no parents or kids were around those vehicles. Everybody was gone. No mink-coat moms, no dads in Cads. Only one light on in the building now, and that had been around front.

The dance instructor?

Did he *live* on the premises, as well? That seemed unlikely but not impossible.

I again nosed the Pinto out of the lot, turning left, heading down the hill. I turned around in a drive and came up and parked opposite the dance studio's parking lot entrance. I had barely done this when another car pulled in just ahead of me and parked.

The Bonneville.

Shit fuck hell, as the nun said when she hammered her thumb.

I just sat there with my nine mil in my hand, draped across my lap, wondering if I'd screwed the pooch already. The Bonneville's driver's side door opened and the big red-haired red-bearded quilt-jacketed apparition that was Mateski—still in those tinted glasses!—got out, and my hand tightened on the nine mil grip. Then, once again, he climbed in the back of the Bonneville.

I waited five minutes, five very long minutes, then pulled out and drove off. When I parked next, after doing another circling-around number, I was just around the corner from Mateski, parked a few spaces beyond where his Bonneville had originally been, where I could just catch a glimpse of the Pontiac's grillwork.

Perhaps three minutes later, a car's bright headlights made me wince—*brights in town? What the hell!* The vehicle was going fairly fast, probably pushing forty, and as it roared through the residential intersection, I saw two things—a pretty blonde teenager behind the wheel, and that she was driving that baby blue Mustang.

Would Mateski follow?

Was the blonde, or maybe one of her parents, the target?

I started the car, just in case. Anyway, I could use the heat.

But the Bonneville stayed put.

So did I, and I left the motor running because I was cold and hungry and tired, and gradually getting to be not cold anymore was about all I could do about any of that.

He was still parked there at three in the morning when I left, heading to the 24-hour delicacies offered at Denny's. Like I said, I was hungry, and I would then head to the Holiday Inn, because I was tired. These are the things we settle for when we are hungry and tired.

Anyway, I'd had a busy day.

I'd bought some Louis L'Amour paperbacks, and I'd flirted with a desk clerk, and had a pleasant and illuminating conversation with a mom in a mink coat.

I'd also, almost certainly, figured out who Mateski's target was.

A dance studio instructor.

Mr. Roger.

No "s."

TWO

A week of surveillance followed.

Mostly it was as boring as shadowing Mateski to and from those antiques shops. Maybe a little more so. I will spare you the details and provide the highlights, since much of it was Mateski in his Bonneville staking out the old skating-rink-turned-dance-studio. This required him moving his car periodically, so that it never sat too long in front of any one house. With VALE DANCE STUDIO on a corner, that gave him—and me, hopscotching similarly in my Pinto—a variety of blocks, streets, and sides of those streets to choose from.

Trickiest thing for me was trying to make sure Mateski didn't notice me moving my car each time he did his. But I managed it.

One person can't maintain a twenty-four-hour surveillance. So Mateski's technique, which was standard on two-man hit teams, was to work a couple of three-to-four-hour sessions a day, separated by several hours. As the days passed, by starting and stopping these sessions at various intervals, the entire twenty-four hours got covered, several times. And it also allowed for meals and calls of nature.

This explains why the passive half of these teams usually spent as much as two weeks nailing down the target's patterns, and rarely less than one.

What became apparent within the first several days was that Roger Vale rarely left his studio. Groceries were delivered. An occasional pizza was delivered, too, and once Chinese. He appeared to be a recluse, though your average recluse doesn't teach dance and have scores of teenage girls entering and leaving his domain for every-other-day after-school classes, with private lessons on the off evenings, a lengthy Saturday morning class, and more private lessons till five.

Keeping track of all the junior high and high school girls that went in and out of that big black bunker of a dance studio was impossible. Ditto their well-off parents picking them up.

A week of this, and I had not yet seen Vale himself. He had not stuck his head out once. At least I didn't think so. I couldn't be sure since I didn't know what he looked like. Mateski knew, but I couldn't exactly ask him, could I?

On the other hand, I had seen that little blonde in the blue Mustang plenty of times, and got several nice looks at her, in fact. She was petite but curvy, the kind of cheerleader they reserve for the top of the pyramid. From a distance, I couldn't make her age—she looked like she could have been as young as fourteen—but the way she seemed always on her own, tooling around in that sporty little rod, I figured her for a senior or at least a junior.

She was also the only indication—other than Vale's apparent reluctance to leave his castle—that anything funny was going on. Not funny ha ha, but funny business, as in a dance instructor maybe banging one of his teenage charges. I wondered what the legal age of consent was in Missouri. Always good to know.

Did I mention she had a vanity license plate? Well, she did, and you are going to love this: SALLY. Yes, the dance instructor's favorite student was Mustang Sally.

And it was fair to say she was his favorite—she stayed for half an hour to an hour after class, and on two occasions slipped inside after private lessons, staying till ten once, and eleven-something twice. Her parents obviously did not have her on a short leash. More like no leash at all.

The kicker was Sunday. Mateski had started his stakeout around eleven A.M., apparently anticipating that our reclusive dance instructor might poke his head out of his cave on what was after all a sunny, less chilly morning, and actually enjoy a day off.

Vale enjoyed his day off, all right, but like the pizza and Chinese, he took home delivery. Little Mustang Sally showed around noon, at the front entrance, with a big bag of Colonel Sanders in one hand and a plump bag labeled STOCKWELL HOME VIDEO in the other. Chicken breast and movies, right at your door. There's a franchise worth investing in.

During that week, nothing much else of import occurred. I remained flirty and friendly with that big-hair blonde desk clerk, when she was on duty, but stayed away off duty. I had come to my senses. No fooling around on the job. Focus, man, focus. That was something smart that I did.

Something smart that Mateski did was, on the fourth day of surveillance, go and get a haircut. He had the wild red fright wig trimmed to businessman length, got rid of the matching beard, and sported a spare pair of glasses minus the rust-color lenses. Maybe he wasn't an imbecile. He had effectively become a different person by mid-week—including clothes conservative enough for a Mormon going door to door—and halved the possibility of being spotted.

I'd have to remember that one.

Now it was exactly a week since I'd first arrived in Stockwell. Mateski and I were both parked very nearly where we'd been that first night, as a few parents waited with engines running to pick up their girls out front. Suddenly Mateski, who for four hours had been at his post—albeit in several different spots, moving the Bonneville as before—started up his engine and pulled out and appeared to drive away.

I waited a few beats, then swung out after him. It took not long at all to determine that he was heading to a bar downtown that he liked to frequent—the Golden Spike. It was a shitkicker dive that sat on its own half a block with a big parking lot that was frequently pretty full. Tonight was no exception.

From across the street where I'd pulled in at a mini-mart, I watched as Mateski left the Bonneville in that lot and headed inside to reward himself, leaving his suit coat in the car and loosening his tie. Miller Time.

So I drove back to the big black bunker perched on that hilltop like a fortress guarding the surrounding residential neighborhood. Following Mateski to his favorite local watering hole and returning had taken all of seven minutes. I made the sharp turn into the Vale Dance Studio parking lot, where again twenty-some expensive rides were waiting for their dancing daughters.

Now and then you catch a break, and I caught a good one. Small, but good. That same mink-coat mom was getting out of her Buick Riviera coupe with its vinyl roof to head over to the short flight of cement steps up to the rear doors of the dance studio.

I hopped out of the Pinto and caught up with her, where at the bottom of the stairs she had paused to take one last drag of her latest smoke before sending it spark-spitting into the night. A few other parents were heading up there, as well.

"Well, hello," I said, falling in next to her. The cement steps were wide enough for that.

"We meet again," she said pleasantly, just a little promise or maybe tease in her tobacco-husky voice. "What brings you back? You're not lost again, are you?"

She'd gathered from my questions last time that I wasn't another parent, though I was hoping anybody who noticed me—though Mateski was no risk at the moment—might make that assumption.

"I'm a writing a story about the arts in small Missouri towns. For the *St. Louis Sun*."

"Reporter, huh?"

"Not exactly Woodward or Bernstein. I do puff pieces."

We were at the top of the stairs now. Several other parents moved around us as we stopped and chatted, though nobody went in yet. Just milled, half a dozen of them—four mothers, two dads, expensive coats. Music inside—"One Singular Sensation," a recording with no vocals—meant practice was still on. Even though her breath was already smoking in the cold, my mink mom was getting a pack of cigarettes out of her purse for a fresh one.

Yes, Virginia Slims. You've come a long way, baby. I bet that's what they said at the door to the cancer clinic. "You know, I could help you out on that," she said, meaning the non-existent article. "I'm very active in the local arts scene."

"That'd be great."

As she extended her leather-gloved right hand, she left the cigarette in her mouth, where it bobbed like she was a blackjack dealer in an illegal game. "Betty Stone. My husband travels. You're at the Holiday Inn, right?"

That was pretty direct.

"Right. John Quarry. Nice to meet you, Mrs. Stone."

"Betty....*Ah*, there's Mr. Roger."

She had turned her head toward the door, where finally the turtle was sticking its head out of its shell.

"Hel-*lo*, everybody," he said, leaning out with one hand on the door, flashing a wide white dazzling smile in a narrow tan face. Handsome in a hooded-eye fashion, with short black hair, heavy black eyebrows and a well-trimmed Tom Selleck mustache.

About my height, trimly muscular in black t-shirt, tights and Capezios.

"Come on in, come in," he said, almost blatantly swishy, I thought. He held the door open for the waiting parents. "It *is* still frigid out there, isn't it? Brrrrrr."

Everybody piled in, including me. We were backstage, but the rear curtains were open, so the stage itself spread out before us, beyond which theater seats extended into darkness made more pronounced by bright footlights. Girls ranging in age from thirteen to eighteen were twirling around doing ballet poses and jazz dance stances, all in tights and ballet slippers. The tights were red or blue, with only one girl in white—the petite pretty Mustang Sally herself, who had a whistle around her neck like a football coach, her tawny blonde tresses a frizzy mane.

So was she his assistant? On closer look, she was closer to eighteen than thirteen—a favorite, a star performer, who had been elevated to first mate on this ship? Although looking at Roger Vale, I didn't think he was mating with anybody, at least not of Sally's sex. That Sunday afternoon must have been strictly Colonel Sanders and VHS. A waste of a Sunday afternoon, if you asked me.

"*Ladies!*" Vale said, moving among them with an athletic grace, despite making a shooing motion as if he were guiding chickens to their coop. "Ladies! Dressing rooms, please. I have a parents' meeting to attend to."

Though she didn't blow the whistle, Sally helped herd the girls to either side of the stage, the younger girls (in blue) going left, the older ones (in red) heading right, a glorious giggling array of slender legs and high hair and perky breasts, nipple nodules fighting tight fabric. And speaking of tight, so were my shorts.

There, I've done it. You've lost respect for me.

Now Vale motioned toward the parents, bringing them—us—in around him, huddling. He was a born director, this guy.

"Now," he said, over-enunciating, "Sally has handouts for the recital next month, with instructions and guidelines and everything you'll need for the trip. It's an overnighter, so we need not just drivers but chaperones. Everybody understand that? Good!"

He was damn near hamming the sibilant effeminacy. He seemed obviously gay, maybe too much so. That could be a good cover for a heterosexual male to get close to impressionable, malleable young girls without alarming their parents.

Vale went on with more information about the upcoming recital in Hannibal next month, answering questions about wardrobe and food allowances and so on. This took about fifteen minutes, after which the girls began to emerge from their respective wings, all bundled up in fall and winter coats, the junior high girls still giggling, the high school girls paired off in confidential conversations.

Some girls went on out to meet parents waiting below in cars, while others joined parents from the recital trip committee, though a few lasses lingered in private confabs while parents waited patiently. My presence among this dwindling contingent had been noted by Vale, who was approaching me with a wary smile.

"I don't believe we've been introduced," he said. Not quite so overtly gay. "You must be one of the dads I haven't met yet."

"No, actually—"

Betty Stone, who'd been at my side through the meeting, said brightly, "This is John Quarry, Roger. He's a journalist, doing a story about small towns and the arts for a St. Louis paper."

"The *Sun*," I said with a nod.

Nice of her to come to my rescue.

Vale smiled, teeth very white under the thick dark mustache. His tan may have come from a bottle, judging by its orange-ish tinge.

"Welcome, Mr. Quarry," he said, and extended his hand.

I shook it. Firm. Confident.

Betty, rounding up her two girls, gave me a smile accompanied by a twinkle in her dark eyes that said, *Aren't I nice and worth knowing?*

I nodded at her, she nodded at me, and then she was gone, and suddenly so was everybody else, except for the little blonde, who was still circling in her white tights. She seemed vaguely irritated, but she was extremely pretty, her features delicate. Even her pert breasts seemed irritated, nips pointing scoldingly at me.

"Will you be needing anything more tonight, Mr. Vale?" she asked. Her voice was high and young, her expression pouty.

"No, thank you, Sally. You've been most helpful."

"I'm glad," she said, just vaguely snippy.

She went off somewhere, and Vale grinned. The contrast of dark mustache and white teeth was almost startling.

"Sally's a little possessive," he said quietly, a priest reflecting on a troublesome parishioner.

"Girls will be girls," I said.

"Won't they? So, Mr. Quarry, how can I help you? We could set up a time to talk."

"If you're free now, we can get this out of the way. If you can spare, say, half an hour?"

"I can do that. If you don't mind sitting and talking to me when I'm still all sweaty."

I shrugged. "I can wait while you shower."

"No, I don't think that's necessary. I don't mind if you don't."

"Very generous of you."

Little Sally, swathed in a white fur coat, moved through without a word and exited into the night.

"Cute kid," I said. "What's she, a senior?"

"Yes. Very talented. She's my right hand."

He went over and, with a twist, locked the deadbolt. I'm no genius with lock picks, but I could have opened that thing in thirty seconds.

He returned and said, "We can talk in my quarters."

Interesting way to put it—quarters. Not office or even room.

"That'd be great," I said.

He turned off the footlights and a few others, then hit a switch that brought up subdued lighting in the audience area beyond. Soon I was following him up the slightly sloping center aisle.

He had a towel around his neck as he led the way. "This used to be a skating rink, you know."

"I heard that."

"When I bought the building, I figured I better live here as well. To get a little bang from the buck."

"Ah."

Then we were on a slightly raised area by the double doors of the entrance. Just inside the glass doors, a ticket booth faced a coat check window. The lobby, where we stood under a single yellowish light, was modest. On either side—where kids once rented skates, and bought popcorn and pop—black walls had been dropped, home to big frames displaying posters of upcoming and past events. Doors to these facing rooms were painted black, too, even the knobs, and all but disappeared.

He gestured to the room at our left. "That's where I sleep." Then he nodded to the right, before heading that way. "This is where I do business, but also relax."

I followed him in. The walls were a light pink, the one at my right engulfed by a many-shelved media center—high-end turntable, cassette tape player, assorted speakers, voluminous LPs, cassette tapes, pre-recorded videotapes, a 24-inch TV, a Betamax VCR. At my left was a kitchenette with cabinets, a counter, a fridge and a fifties Formica table and chairs. Tucked against the wall of the door we'd come in was an ancient rolltop desk, open to reveal stacks of bills and music and assorted paperwork, a swivel chair in attendance, over-seen by an array of wall-hung framed photos of what I gathered were local dance recitals Vale had directed.

Against the far wall was a modern brown-leather couch with a pair of matching easy chairs separated by a low-riding coffee table with a big hardcover book called *Broadway Musicals*. Speaking of which, over the couch hung framed posters of recent shows—*Pippin*, *A Chorus Line*, *Follies*, *Dreamgirls*. This area had a multi-color shag rug on the old wood floor. Very neat, this space was. With the exception of the desk's clutter, it was more like the set for a play than somewhere anybody lived. But the stage was at the other end of the building, right?

He rubbed his face with the towel, wadded and tossed it on the Formica table, and headed toward the refrigerator. "Some-thing to drink? I have bottled water, orange juice, Diet Coke. I don't drink alcohol, I'm afraid."

"Diet Coke is fine."

"Good choice." He got us two cans and brought mine to me. "This is *so* much better than that Tab shit, don't you think?"

Still in my fleece-lined leather jacket, I was standing at the edge of the shag carpet. "Yeah, I could never stand that stuff," I said, taking the can of pop.

We were bonding now—he had said "shit" in front of me and everything.

He gestured toward the couch and I sat, while he took the nearby overstuffed easy chair. It had a little side table with a coaster for his Diet Coke. He leaned forward, knees akimbo, folded hands draped between them. "What can I do for you, Mr. Quarry?"

I was getting out of the coat, and as I did, I brought the nine millimeter out.

Not surprisingly, he sat back, dark eyes no longer hooded, and his hands went up, chest high, palms out, as if I were a hold-up man.

"You don't need to be concerned about me," I said pleasantly, resting the nine mil on the coffee table, then tossed the jacket on the cushion next to me. "But there's somebody else you *do* need to be worried about."

"What the hell is the meaning of this?" His tone was hushed, with nothing even vaguely swishy in it now.

I squinted at him. "Listen, are you a fag or what?"

"That's an offensive term."

"You're right. I apologize. Are you?"

"Gay? Yes. Why? What the hell does that have to do with anything?"

"I don't know yet. Maybe nothing. But at least you've dropped the phony flamer routine."

He was still sitting back but his hands were on his thighs now. The gun on the coffee table was offputting, but he was handling it well.

He said, "It, uh…comforts some of the parents to think I'm a harmless queen. This is a very backward part of the country, you know."

"Not as backward as some of it." I gestured toward the theater beyond this enclosed space. "You have a prosperous clientele. Some may even be well-educated."

He frowned at me, his eyes searching. "Is this some kind of shakedown? You're barking up the wrong tree, let me tell you. I'm not wealthy by any means."

"I imagine you do all right, considering what you can get away charging these rich yokels. But I'm not here to shake you down, Mr. Vale."

"Why the…why that *thing*, then?"

He meant the gun. It was old and not pretty.

"I was just making a point," I said, but I left it there. "I'm here to help you."

His lip curled in a slight smile; he had stopped being quite so scared. "I'm not interested in selling Shaklee."

That made me laugh. "No, I suppose you aren't." I leaned forward. "Look, I apologize for the melodramatics. I needed to get your attention."

"I appreciate good showmanship."

"Yeah, well, this isn't playtime. It's very real. Somebody wants you dead. I'm here to help you stay alive."

He frowned again, only this time something in the dark eyes said he understood why what I'd just said wasn't ridiculous— that it made terrible sense.

But he said, "I thought the melodramatics were over."

"We're way past that stage, actually."

"Who are you?"

"Call me Quarry. No mister necessary. I'm an investigator of sorts."

"Of sorts? Not police?"

"Not police. Private, but not licensed. I followed a man here who was sent to ascertain your habits. Your pattern. He's doing that to provide information to another man, who will arrive any day now. To kill you."

His eyes were hard now, though his chin was quivering. If he didn't know what I was talking about, he'd have dismissed that last bit as more melodrama. He didn't. He sure didn't.

"This is sounding like a shakedown, after all," he said, but weakly.

"No. I'll leave if you aren't interested in my services."

"What…what are your services?"

"For a fee, I'll remove those two men."

"Remove?"

"Kill them."

He smiled, but it was an awful sideways thing. "You say that like…you're saying you'll wash my car."

"You do have a nice car. I always wanted a Corvette. Indicates you can afford my services, that's for sure."

His eyes were racing with thought. "You'll…kill them…both? The one who is…watching me, and the other who will…what, show up some time soon, and…?"

"Kill you. Yes. It wouldn't be hard. I know you've sequestered yourself in this concrete bomb shelter, but that just makes it easier. This place is very easy to break into. Do you have a gun?"

"Of course I don't have a gun!"

I sipped my Diet Coke, then put the can back on its coaster next to the nine mil. "Yet you aren't shocked when I say someone wants you dead."

"No…no, I'm not."

"Tell me about it, Roger. All right if I call you Roger?"

"Yes." He licked his lower lip. Dark eyes were racing under the darker slashes of eyebrow. "It's…it's the missing Stockwell girl."

"What missing Stockwell girl?"

Another frown, irritated now. "*The* missing Stockwell girl. Candace Stockwell, daughter of Lawrence Stockwell, grand-daughter of Clarence Stockwell."

"Ah…I take it this is the family that the town is named for."

He nodded. "It goes back to when Stockwell was the Buggy Whip Capital of America."

"You're kidding."

His frown deepened. "I'm not in a joshing frame of mind, Mr. Quarry."

"Just Quarry is fine. Buggy whips?"

Weary sigh. "There was a big demand at one time, and a factory here, and the Stockwells made their money at it, before it went bust after Henry Ford came along. All that early money put them in banking, and from banking came insurance, and if you've driven around downtown, you know that every other business is a Stockwell this or that."

"Not just named after the town?"

"No. The Stockwell family doesn't allow that name to be attached anywhere but to their enterprises. Or at least that's what I understand. I've only lived here two years." He was breathing heavily.

"Take your time, Roger. Take it easy."

"Candy…Candace…was a very beautiful girl, lovely face, lovely figure. And very talented. She was easily the most talented dancer I've ever taught here, or possibly anywhere else. Even better than Sally, although Sally is better at ballet. Jazz dance was Candy's forte."

"Nice girl, Candy?"

He rolled his eyes. "Actually…if I may be forgiven? Candy Stockwell was a little slut. No. A *gigantic* slut. Spoiled, selfish, and, well…she was what we called, back when I was in school, loose. Oh, she had a steady boyfriend, captain of the football team…but the rest of the team had her, too. Everybody wanted some, but *this* Candy, I assure you, she was definitely *not* sweet."

"Okay. She put out. But why all the past tense? Is the girl dead?"

He shrugged, threw up his hands. "Who knows? She's gone. But plenty of people around here *assume* she's dead. More than that, they assume she was *murdered*."

"Why isn't the assumption that she's a runaway?"

"Why would she do that? Since her mother died, she had her daddy wrapped around her little finger. She drove a Datsun 280ZX. Kept whatever hours she chose. Hired her friends to do her homework, and no teacher in town would dare call her on it, or any cheating she might do. No. Her life was the best gig a teenage girl ever had."

"Somebody thinks you killed her."

"Yes."

"Why?"

He sighed. Shook his head. Shrugged helplessly. "Well, she framed me, Quarry. Unwittingly, I believe. But she framed me."

"Explain."

"She used to come on to me. She loved to tease me, and tell me that I wasn't gay, I was probably bi, and if I just found the right girl, I'd know that. *She* was that girl, she said. She just *knew* she could turn me. She wanted a chance to try, anyway."

"And you didn't give her one."

He nodded glumly. "But then she wrote about me in her diary, in excruciating, pornographic detail, describing some imaginary affair, with all kinds of…" He sighed, shook his head. "…wild tales of anal sex and whips and chains and God knows what."

"And when she disappeared, that diary was found…and believed."

"By *some*." He sat forward again. "I have a good deal of support in this community, Mr. Quarry…Quarry…*despite* the Stockwells. For the last two years, I've helped prepare local girls entering various pageants, and the first group I coached, one girl was first runner-up in Miss Missouri, and another was

Miss Teen Missouri and went on to be second runner-up in national."

"Impressive," I said, not giving a shit.

He scowled, not at me, at a memory. "But the Stockwells, particularly *Old Man* Stockwell…Clarence, the grandfather, the senile old prick…he *accused* me. Slandered me right in the pages of the *Stockwell Sentinel*."

"You couldn't sue or anything?"

"Not in this town—and that was just the beginning of it! The old man pressured the police to bring me in for questioning. It never went anywhere, of course. I had an alibi, and I even allowed the police, without a warrant, to go through my quarters here. They found nothing. I was completely cleared."

I huffed a laugh. "But that wasn't good enough for the Stockwell family."

"No. They brought in private detectives, who spent weeks invading my privacy, but also came up empty. That didn't satisfy the Stockwells, either." He shook his head, rubbed his mustache nervously. "I've thought about simply packing up and moving on, but that might seem an…an admission of guilt, and I didn't *do* anything, Quarry, not a goddamn thing."

"You think the grandfather took out a contract?"

He shook his head in a gesture of uncertainty. "He may seem the most likely, but it could be Candy's father…her mother is deceased, did I mention that?…or that aunt of hers, who is wild as Candy was. Wilder. I've had anonymous death threats on the phone, veiled threats from her married choir director, and not so-veiled ones from that boyfriend, an oaf named Rodney Pettibone. Who in the twentieth century is named Pettibone, for God's sake? And why would a parent add insult to injury with 'Rodney'? But…a contract killing, is that what we're talking about?"

"Yes."

He squinted at the thought of it. "How would ordinary people be able to take out a...*contract* on someone's life?"

"Doesn't sound like the Stockwells are all that ordinary. A rich family like that may have all kinds of shady associations in their past. Anyway, people in bars offer other people in bars fifty bucks to kill a spouse they hate, or a boss. Happens all the time."

"But this isn't fifty dollars in a bar."

"No. You're right about that. This is high-priced talent."

He cocked his head. "How much would someone have paid to...?"

"At least as much as I intend to ask of you."

"Which is...how much?"

"Ten thousand dollars. Five now, or anyway as soon as possible. Five more when I've finished the job."

He thought about it.

"Sell your Corvette if you have to," I said.

"I still owe on it." But then: "I can manage that much. But it strikes me...don't I *still* have a problem?" Again, the dark eyes probed me, not at all hooded now. "Someone out there will still want to kill me, even after you've...removed these...God, am I really saying this? Hitmen."

I nodded. "That's another ten grand."

"What is?"

"Me finding out *who* wants you dead."

"And...removing them, too?"

"And removing them, too."

He sat and thought about it some more.

Then he sighed and said, "Will you take a check?"

THREE

Well, of course I told my new client that this was a cash only business, and he said he could have the money by tomorrow. I told him to get it together and I'd stop by sometime in the next few days to get it. I couldn't be any more specific than that because my schedule was determined by Mateski's. Didn't mention the name Mateski to Vale, obviously. All he needed to know was that people were coming to kill him, and I was going to stop it. For cash.

And over the weekend, Mateski's surveillance technique of staking Vale out for three or four hours at a time, at alternating intervals, continued. Mostly days, now. It was obvious nothing much happened late at night, with Vale never venturing from the black bunker. The dance instructor was clearly not going anywhere. Mateski was probably smiling by now, figuring he and his partner—whoever that partner might be—had a sitting duck of a target.

Then on Sunday Mateski threw me a real curve. Though yesterday had been a day shift, my surveillance subject did not emerge from his cabin at the Rest Haven Court till late morning, at which time he drove to the nearby Denny's for breakfast. Despite his shorter-haired, clean-shaven appearance, he suddenly looked more himself—back in the big-frame orange-tinted glasses, wearing his quilted ski jacket over blue-plaid flannel shirt with new jeans and Hush Puppy boots.

Was he trying for a third demeanor as he headed into the last lap of his surveillance duties?

Something the fuck was definitely up, and I was already

tightening my loose tail, going ahead and having a burger at the counter where I could keep an eye on him sitting solo in a corner booth. He was in no hurry to get anywhere, taking up space and downing refills of coffee while he sat reading a door-stop of a paperback—*North and South* by John Jakes. I noticed the title heading to the john, breezing by him.

He was still reading when I headed out to the parking lot and waited in the Pinto to see what he did next. Maybe he was taking a day off. That wasn't typical for somebody working the passive role in our business, but maybe he needed a break—we had put in nine days straight, the two of us. Christ, I was starting to feel like we were in this together.

When he finally emerged and got into the Bonneville, I picked up the tail and suddenly was in a rerun of how this trip began—he stopped at an antiques shop downtown. There were five other such shops taking up most of one side of the street on one of the shopping district's four blocks.

I didn't follow him inside. Across the way was a cluster of gift shops that were obviously just hobbling along during the off-season. Among them was a too-cute "old-fashioned" soda fountain, where I went in and took a table in the window and sipped a chocolate malt through a straw, like Archie waiting for Veronica. The pleasantly plump blonde waitress who after while brought my check had a name tag that said BETTY. I shit you not.

"That's sure a whole bunch of antiques shops," I said to her stupidly.

"Antiques Row," she said brightly. Nice kid. Pretty. Maybe oughta work someplace with less calories, though.

"Must be a real draw in the summer," I said.

"Not just then. It's a year-round destination for antiquers from all over."

Distracted for a moment by how awful a word "antiquers" was, I said, "Really? Just for that handful of shops?"

She leaned in and pointed. She smelled good. Like hot fudge. "Down on the corner there? It's one of the biggest antique malls in the Midwest. Why, a real dyed-in-the-wool antiquer could spend hours in there."

Which is just what Mateski did. Long enough for me to start and finish another Louis L'Amour—over two hours in just that corner building, and another two in the other shops, popping out occasionally with a God-awful painting in tow or some other primitive gee-gaw, including a small stool that looked like a slow kid pounded it out right before flunking shop class.

Lovingly, he packed these horrific gems away in his trunk and in his back seat and even in the rider's seat.

He was indeed taking a day off, but not to relax—rather, he was doing some buying for his other business. After all, he'd told his employees back in Woodstock that he was off on a picking trip. Couldn't go home empty-handed, could he?

And going home was exactly what he was prepping to do.

I followed him back to the Rest Haven, then watched from the window of my Holiday Inn room as he fussed with his finds in the trunk and back seat, utilizing bubble wrap he'd come up with somehow. But he did not take any of these treasures inside his room, content to leave them in the car, including the easily seen stuff in the back seat.

That made it unlikely he intended to stay the night. He would be on the road soon. His job here was over.

Mine was just beginning.

Just after dusk, I drove to the dance studio and swung into the parking lot. Only the red Corvette was parked there. I left the Pinto next to it, like its ugly cousin, all but ran up the back cement steps, then circled around the building to knock at the front entrance. I hadn't wanted to park out front and ascend all those steps where someone would be more likely to notice.

My first knocks didn't rouse him, so I pounded harder on the steel framing of the glass doors, which were painted out black. I was about to try again when one cracked open and the tanned mustached mug of Roger Vale peeked out at me.

"Quarry," he said, goggling, surprised to see me but also wondering if he should be alarmed.

I brushed by him through the barely opened door and when he had shut and locked it behind me, I said, "What the fuck's the idea, opening the door like that?"

He was in baggy black sweats and sneakers, not the former lithe vision in tights and Capezios. "Well, didn't you *want* in?"

I pointed to the black-painted glass. "You can't see out that door. I could be anybody."

"I'm expecting a pizza!"

"I'm expecting somebody to kill your ass. Look, the guy watching you is wrapping things up. That means the hit will go down in no more than three days, very probably much less."

His eyes widened and his mouth dropped. "Fuck me."

"You, fuck you, if you aren't more cautious. Get my money."

He swallowed. Gestured toward the open door to the room where we'd sat and spoken—the brown-leather couch and the framed Broadway posters visible. "You want to come in and go over things?"

"No. Get my money."

He wasn't sure whether to be offended or frightened. Then he shrugged and disappeared in there, was gone maybe half a minute, returning to hand me a thick envelope.

"Hundred, fifties and twenties," he said. "Like you said."

I stuffed the envelope in the jacket pocket that didn't have a nine millimeter in it. "You need to be more careful. I am on top of this, but you need to be, too."

He nodded and nodded some more.

There was a knock at the door, hard and rattling, and we both jumped like a couple of girls trying out for his class.

"Fuck," we said softly.

Shortly I was edged along the inside wall next to the doors and, as per my whispered instructions, Vale stood plastered to the wall on the other side ("You know, Roger, it's possible to shoot through glass, even if it is painted black").

"Yes," Vale nearly shouted. "What is it?"

"Pizza Hut," a young bored male voice said.

I gave Vale the okay and he reached over and flipped the lock. The kid was allowed in, delivered the pie, got paid, tipped, and went on his way, unaware that a nine mil was in my fist behind my back all the while.

Vale stood there in his sweats with a big flat brown greasy box in his hands. How did he eat pizza like that and stay so fucking slim? Life was not fair.

He said, "Sure you don't want to stay? There's plenty."

"I've stayed too long. Let me out the back."

He did, and I was right—I shouldn't have risked the trip to the dance studio at all. I had wanted to warn Vale and, frankly, get my down payment. But even before I pulled into the Holiday Inn parking lot, I could see the Bonneville was no longer parked in front of Cabin 12.

Fuck me, as my client had said.

Was Mateski already on the way home? Had I somehow missed the requisite meeting between him and his partner? In these post-Broker days, that practice of passive and active conferring face-to-face could have evolved into something else—

with Mateski filling his partner in via Ma Bell maybe, and leaving a notebook at some designated drop.

Shit.

I didn't know who Mateski's partner was. There was a long-shot possibility that the active hitter would be somebody I knew, someone I'd worked with. But that was a short list, particularly compared to the Broker's. I had looked at every photograph in the file, more than once, but it wasn't like I'd memorized all those faces.

This left me shit out of luck—Vale, too. Worse for him, I'll grant you. Me, I could leave Stockwell right now, taking along the dance instructor's five thousand bucks, to make up for all the surveillance I'd sat. And what would be the harm? A dead guy doesn't miss money.

Still, I preferred to earn my fees, and anyway another fifteen grand was at stake. I knew where Mateski was heading—Woodstock, Illinois. He'd probably begin that journey, at least, by heading north on Highway 218, going back the way we came.

With his car full to the brim with that primitive junk, he wasn't heading in some other direction for more buying. No. Woodstock Or Bust. Right now he would only have maybe forty minutes on me.

But there was another possibility, glimmering like heat over asphalt. *Maybe Mateski was still in town.* Maybe he hadn't met with his partner yet, and that meet was scheduled for...*right now.* This evening.

If so, where was that likely to be?

On a Sunday night, the Golden Spike was not hopping. Decent business, but nothing like a Friday or Saturday, or even a week-night. I had been in a hundred of these bars and they were all the same, though they tended to vary on the sleaze scale. The

Spike was about a seven, clean but loud, from the boisterous bullshit of farmers who thought they were ranchers and the hourly workers who thought they were cowboys, to a jukebox blaring Alabama and Rosanne Cash for the younger set and George Jones and Loretta Lynn for the older crowd.

As you came in, the bar was at your left, separated from a row of booths by a half-dozen high-top tables. Maybe half the booths were filled, all but one high-top empty; a third of the bar stools were taken. At the rear were two pool tables, one in use. George Strait was splitting the demographic difference on the jukebox.

I took the stool nearest the door, nobody next to me. The barmaid was a short brick-shithouse highlighted brunette in her early twenties in a glittery purple tank-top cut low enough to encourage generous tips. Some strategies never get old.

She didn't ask what I wanted, just stared across the counter with dark bored eyes.

"Coke," I said.

This she found ridiculous but let her expression say it for her. When she returned with a glass, I was looking past her at the mirror under the array of neon beer signs and behind the row of liquor bottles.

"Run a tab?" she asked me.

I nodded.

"You seem distracted."

Apparently I'd offended her by not looking down her tank-top. "Hard day at the office."

"On Sunday?"

"I'm the new pastor at Calvary United. Saving souls is a bitch."

She shrugged, said, "Explains the Coke," and went away.

In the mirror, I was keeping an eye on the booth on the far end, trying not to be too conspicuous about it. But since Mateski was sitting with his back to me, I didn't have to work very hard at it.

I wasn't surprised to see him, having spotted the Bonneville in the parking lot. No one was across the booth from him. He had a beer in front of him, only a third or so of it gone. Reading again, if you can believe it, holding *North and South* near the booth's little light over the napkin holder.

So he was waiting for somebody.

I sipped Coke. Smiled. And I knew who that somebody was, didn't I? Or I sort of knew. Knew the role of the person, anyway, who would eventually enter that door near my back and go over to sit down with Mateski.

"I'm Jenny," a husky female voice said from the stool next door. "You got a name to go with that nice face?"

My first look at her was in the mirror. I had stopped looking at Mateski and lowered my gaze as my thoughts kicked in, and hadn't noticed her when she edged up onto the stool beside me, a dark lanky girl with unlikely large boobs poured into a black low-cut Harley t-shirt and frayed jeans.

I said, "Got a pretty nice face there your own self."

But it was not a face that I would really call "nice," exactly— sharp, well-defined features framed by a big head of gypsy curls, black with silver streaks; dark thick arching eyebrows, eyes big, an unusual light green, full wide mouth glistening crimson with a real-looking black beauty mark at one corner. High cheekbones, cleft chin. Kind of dark tan that turns leathery in a woman's forties; she wasn't quite there yet.

"Jack," I said. "Jack Quarry."

I could use her for cover, to make my presence here less conspicuous.

She took the hand I offered. Hers was warm. Somewhere between a handshake and a caress.

"You're new in town," she said.

I gave her half a grin, swirled my beverage. "You make it sound like an old western. What am I, a stranger in Dodge?"

She gave me the other half of the grin. "Are you?"

"I guess. You must get your share of strangers around here, Miss Kitty. It's the Little Vacationland of Missouri, right?"

"Not this time of year."

The barmaid rolled her chest and confidence over and deposited a lowball glass of ice and amber fluid before Jenny. The women nodded at each other, like members of opposing sports teams, and the barmaid went away.

"I didn't hear you order," I said.

"Mary Ann knows I always have Jack and Ginger."

"Sounds like *Gilligan's Island*, only with Jack in the middle."

She laughed. Her teeth were handsome but a light yellow. Was that Opium perfume, trying to cover up the tobacco smell on her? How could she afford that shit? Of course, bikers dealt derivatives of that other opium, and she did appear to be a biker chick.

She asked, "What are *you* drinking?"

"Coca-Cola."

"The hard stuff, huh?"

"You don't think cocaine is hard?"

"Honey, they stopped putting cocaine in Coke Cola a long damn time ago."

I liked the way she said that—Coke Cola. She wasn't stupid. In fact, I was pretty sure she was smart.

I shrugged, sipped. "As long as they keep the caffeine in, I'm in. That's *my* drug of choice."

"Ha! That *is* good shit. Where would we all be without black coffee in the morning?"

I gave her a flirty smile. "I wonder where I'll be in the morning?"

"It's early yet. Who can tell?"

Mateski was still reading. His beer was down to a third of a glass now. A waitress came with another for him, and he seemed to be ordering something off the menu. Couldn't blame him—good bar food at the Golden Spike, and I hadn't seen him eat since Denny's. He really seemed to be hunkering in for the duration.

But the duration of what?

Jenny was lighting up a smoke with a silver lighter with a Harley symbol on it. Camel, no filter tip. No Virginia Slims bullshit for this babe. She swung the pack toward me.

"No thanks," I said.

"Don't smoke, huh? Wanna live forever?"

"I have the Olympic trials to worry about."

She chuckled, snapped shut her lighter. It was louder than the jukebox. "You're that good influence I've been trying to avoid all my life."

"Yeah, I think I could straighten you out in a hurry."

She put a hand on my thigh. "You took the words right out of my mouth."

My dick twitched, like a heavy sleeper reacting to an alarm clock. *Down boy*, I told it.

She leaned on an elbow and gave me a wide, nasty smile, gazing at me with translucent green eyes, such lovely eyes to be wearing so much mascara in such a hard face. Lovely face. Probably wrinkled if the lights were up. But they were down.

"What do you do, anyway, Jack?"

"In what sense?"

"In the work sense. Are you employed?"

"Self-employed."

"And you do what?"

I stuck with my cover story. "I'm a journalist. Freelance."

"And what brings you to scenic Stockwell in the dead of winter?"

"It's still fall."

"Felt like winter all week."

"No argument there. I'm working on a story about the local arts scene."

That subject apparently held no interest for her. She blew out more smoke. For a top-heavy gal, she had a bony look, elbow against the bar, half-turned to me with her legs crossed, her knees sharp, the toes of her motorcycle boots the same. How could all those angular bones seem so feminine?

"So you're in town how long, Jack?"

"Maybe a week."

"And you're from where, exactly?"

"Ever live in St. Louis, Jenny?"

"No."

"St. Louis."

"It's a fun town. I've partied there before."

I hid my shock. "Wish I'd run into you. Take you up to my apartment. Show you my etchings."

She frowned at me. "What are etchings, anyway?"

"Fuck if I know."

That got a throaty laugh out of her and her empty glass was automatically replaced by the other bosomy babe.

"What do *you* do, Jenny?"

"Nothing. Whatever the fuck I like. I'm independently wealthy."

"Are you now?"

"You think I'm shitting you? I'm not shitting you."

"Did I say you were shitting me?"

"No, Jack, I don't believe you did. Excuse me. Little girl's room." She slid off the stool and hip-swayed toward the back and the johns. The tits might be fake, but that well-shaped ass was the real deal. Might have been on pistons, the way those cheeks moved up and down.

She wove around the waitress bringing Mateski a plate with burger and fries.

"Hey," somebody said.

Mary Ann.

The barmaid was leaning in, giving me a very generous view down the blouse at the decidedly real thing. The head of my half a hard-on turned toward her.

"You be careful, honey," she said.

"Yeah? Why?"

"That crazy cunt, excuse my French, has screwed every-thing that moves in this town, and a few that were standing still."

"Oh. Well, that discourages me. We don't go in for that kind of thing at Calvary."

"Yeah, I'm sure you don't. But she wasn't lying."

"Huh?"

"She's richer than shit. She's the black sheep of the biggest family in town."

"What, the Stockwells?"

She nodded. "That's Jenny Stockwell you're flirting with."

What the hell?

I said, "So if I marry her I'll be rich, then?"

"She's not the marrying kind. At least not lately. Likes her freedom."

"Kiss and run, huh? That's depressing. I'm only interested in long-term relationships. What time do you get off? And I mean that in the nicest way."

She grinned at me. Her teeth were white. "Okay, smart-ass. Don't listen to me. But will you take just a little friendly advice?"

"Maybe."

"Don't go out in the rain without your rubbers on. You might catch something, and not a cold."

Jenny was nearing the bar as the barmaid gave me a knowing smirk and a raised eyebrow and got lost.

"Let's go outside," Jenny said. A big black purse was slung over an arm; it had a Harley logo, too. "I could use a little air."

Mateski was eating his burger, slowly, still reading.

"Okay," I said.

She took me by the hand and led me out into the parking lot. She escorted me around the side of the building where it was dark, only a single angled row of cars parked between the lot and the next building. I had a feeling this was where the help left their vehicles. There were garbage cans back here, but they were probably empty, because nothing stank.

She pushed me against the side of the Spike. No windows back here. Nice and private, though I could see an occasional car pull out of the lot. Driver and any passengers wouldn't see us unless they looked in their rear-view mirror as they exited. She smothered my mouth with her sticky lipstick-moist lips and her tongue raped the tender space between my upper and lower teeth. It was disgusting. My dick throbbed like a thumb caught in a car door.

Jenny Stockwell—a coincidence? Small town. Possible. Or had I been made? Was she meeting Mateski here? Had she hired the hit on Vale, and was going to confab with both Mateski and his partner? Maybe hired them herself, independently, no middle-man. Did she have a gun in that big black purse? I had one in my fleece-lined jacket....

And yet I still had a raging hard-on.

We necked for a frantic while, then my hands went up under that t-shirt and the breasts were large and perfect and a little hard, probably implants, but I did not give a flying fuck. The nipples were hard as bullets and I didn't care who saw, I tugged that Harley shirt up and transferred the lipstick she left on my face to those big firm globes and the hard tips begged for suckling and I didn't disappoint. She was on her knees then, and unzipped me and unbuttoned me and tugged my shorts down to let the brains of the organization out for some air. It bobbed and pulsed and stared at her like a creature in a Ray Harryhausen movie. She grinned at it, happy as a kid with a brand-new toy, though I was pretty sure she'd seen plenty of previous models; she flicked at it with a forefinger and school-girl giggled as it bobbed up and down.

Then, surprisingly, she said, "Listen, sweetie, I'm a spitter, okay? Just so we got the ground rules."

"Yeah. Sure. Okay."

"I got wet naps in my purse if you want to finish on my face."

"Spitting's fine. I don't offend easily."

Then she was gobbling the thing, taking it deep, a messy, slurpy, saliva-heavy, nasty fucking process that had me drunker than anybody inside. I almost missed it when a car came in the wrong way and I recognized the guy behind the wheel, who disappeared from view pulling into the lot to park.

"Honey," she said, her hand working me, "you're losing it. Concentrate."

"Yeah. Yeah."

I didn't know him. I'd never worked with him. But I remembered him from the Broker's file. I had studied that face long and hard because it was a face I never wanted to see in the flesh. It was one name on the list that I would never, under any circumstances, pursue.

She was working me with her hand. "Hmmm, good boy. You're doing fine, sugar. Just fine."

Then she took me back into her mouth and worked her magic till I was shivering and shuddering like a guy in his fucking death throes and when she went over to discreetly spit me out, behind the garbage cans, I felt she conducted herself with considerable dignity.

I'd put myself back together by the time she returned. She was using a little breath-freshener spray, which she then slipped into her purse. Her lipstick was gone but otherwise her make-up looked fine. Industrial strength mascara.

"That was fun," she said. "You have a good time, honey?"

"Sure did."

"You wanna see me again while you're town, I'm in the book. Jenny Stockwell."

We shook hands.

"Keep in touch," she said. "I got somewhere else you might like to stick that thing." And grabbed my crotch in a friendly way.

"No problem," I said.

We held hands as she walked me back in. Our bar stools were waiting. Mary Ann brought me a fresh Coke and Jenny another Jack and Ginger.

Mateski had been joined in the bar by a man I knew as Reed Farrell. He was a very well-dressed man for this down-home a venue—a sharp charcoal suit and thin emerald tie, a cadaverous undertaker of a man, with a long narrow face that was baby's-butt smooth, as if it had never experienced an emotion. His hair was cut very short, his eyebrows thick but trimmed back, his complexion blister pale, with slitted eyes that blinked in slow motion. He sat with his hands folded, a mixed drink before him as Mateski leaned across the booth's table, quietly filling him in.

Remember how I said there was one guy in my business who specialized in torture?

Or were you ahead of me?

FOUR

When I say torture, I don't mean anything psychological and not even using increasing degrees of discomfort and violence to make somebody talk. Sure, I've put a bullet in a kneecap to pry loose information, but I don't consider that torture. Just expedience.

The kind of torture Reed Farrell administered was not designed to make you talk—more like scream. My late, longtime back-up guy, Boyd, had worked with Farrell once and swore he never would again. Boyd hadn't witnessed any of the rough stuff, but later got freaked out to learn that the hit he'd set up resulted in some middle-echelon Cincinnati mob guy having his fingers, toes and dick cut off systematically with garden shears, then dumped to die, bleeding out of those various new orifices.

Seemed Farrell had been a field medic in Vietnam and picked up tricks from the Cong—he could make punishment of that kind last without the victim passing out or going into the kind of shock that robbed the client of the satisfaction of the target's suffering.

Mob hits were something I had occasionally done, and that was true for everybody who worked through the Broker, but those jobs were the minority. Mostly we disposed of crooked business partners, pesky business rivals, cheating wives, cheating husbands, and other civilians who had displeased some important somebody.

Imagine mob guys feeling they needed to bring in a guy like Farrell—that their own in-house expertise for mayhem just wasn't up to the task of making some asshole suffer sufficiently. Kind of says it all.

This wasn't just a guy skilled with a gun and/or a knife, or an expert in staging believable accidents; this was (as the Broker's file detailed) an individual skilled in such arts as bone-breaking, freezing, live burial, castration, toe/fingernail removal, flaying, limb-sawing, burning, and scalping; a specialist able to prolong a victim's misery before death for many hours and even days, skilled with such esoteric devices as cattle prods, thumbscrews, cat o' nine tails, branding iron, Tucker Telephone (don't ask), and Picana (ditto).

"You men," Jenny was saying, lighting up another Camel.

"Huh?" I said, shifting my eyes to her in the barroom mirror from watching the back-booth meeting between the torturer and the antiques dealer.

"You shoot your wad," she said, curling her crimson-lipsticked upper lip (she had redone her makeup in the Spike ladies' room), "and then get all quiet. All morose."

"Maybe I'm just satisfied."

I hadn't seen any documents passed between them. Maybe I'd missed that, since Farrell was already in that booth when I'd returned. But there was no manila envelope or folder or notebook on the table, and almost always the surveillance guy turned over extensive notes to the hitter. Maybe it was beside Farrell on the booth seat, blocked from view.

Jenny said, "You intrigue me."

"I'm an intriguing sort of guy."

"You wouldn't want to come see *my* etchings, would you? I got a nice house. Nice bed. No kids. No husbands."

"Sounds lonely."

"Just *terrible* lonely. I could use some company."

Was she part of this? Had I just been invited to my own

murder? Silly as that might sound, keep in mind: I was sitting there looking in the barroom mirror at a guy whose definition of Iron Maiden wasn't a heavy metal band.

I turned my gaze to her and smiled, gently. I touched the red-nailed hand that didn't have a cigarette in it. "Sugar, you drained the company right out of me. But I'm hanging around town all week. I *do* want to get together."

"If that's the brush-off, you have nice technique."

I shook my head. "Not the brush-off. You intrigue me, too."

The gypsy hair and the dark tan and the wide scarlet mouth and the green translucence of her eyes really did intrigue me. So did the sadness behind her flip slutty manner, and the intelligence in that beautiful, time-and-cigarette-ravaged face. If she didn't want to kill me, marrying her might be an option. She had money and she could suck the chrome off a '57 Chevy fender. Who could ask for more in a female?

She got into her purse and took out a black felt-tip pen. "Give me your hand," she said.

I complied.

She wrote a series of numbers across my wrist. "That's my phone number. Don't call before eleven A.M."

I glanced at the black numbers on my skin. "That was unnecessary. You said you were in the book."

"Well, that will remind you." She tossed a five on the bar and gathered her things.

She'd had four of those Jack and Gingers. I knew I should drive her home, but I needed to keep an eye on Farrell and Mateski, who were still deep in conversation, former listening, latter chattering.

"Listen," I said, "I can run you home, but I can't come in. I'm meeting somebody here later and have to get right back."

She slid off the stool. "Another woman, already?" She nodded toward the barmaid, down serving somebody. "Hate to break your heart, but Mary Ann has a boyfriend."

"I'm not surprised, and it's not another woman. It's an interview for my story. Really."

She shrugged elaborately. She was a little drunk. "You don't owe me anything, Jack. You can go home and wash my number off and no big deal. Of course, late at night, every now and then, you'll remember that hummer out by those garbage cans, and you'll wonder what you missed out on. I'll give you a hint— they call me Snapper Jenny. Wouldn't you like to know why?"

"I think I might know."

She grinned. Those teeth were yellowish but it was a hell of a smile. "I bet you do, Jack. I just bet you do."

She leaned in and kissed me on the cheek, leaving lipstick behind. I swiveled on the stool to watch her go. Long limbs, bony kind of frame, but such a nice round ass.

Then she was out the door in a blast of cold air.

Mary Ann in her purple tank-top materialized, rubbed the lipstick off my cheek with a drink napkin, and asked, "Another Coke?"

"Just freshen this one, would you?"

She nodded, and when she came back with it, gave me the cleavage lean-in, saying, "You and Jenny have a good time outside, Pastor?"

"I ministered to her needs."

"I'll just bet you did. I bet she got down on her knees and prayed."

"You're half-right."

She didn't try topping that, just threw me a smirk and wandered down to needle some other customer.

Farrell was sliding out of the booth. He paused to smooth his sharp suit and shake hands with Mateski, then strode in my direction; but his eyes weren't on me, or anything specifically.

They were cold hard unblinking orbs, small black buttons sewn on a ragdoll's face.

That nicely tailored suit did not allow for any document to be tucked away in a side pocket, and he wasn't carrying anything. Had Mateski given him chapter-and-verse out loud, in that back booth? With no need for sharing his surveillance notes, and for Farrell just to remember? That seemed very damn doubtful.

The slender hitman let in some more brisk air in as he went out—the temperature was falling—and through the Spike's front window I saw him stroll to a nondescript gray vehicle. When I'd seen him pull into the Spike's lot, I hadn't discerned the make, but now I did: a Chevy Cavalier, four-door, an '80 or '81. Nothing special, which made sense, because Farrell probably bought it for cash at some shady used lot like I had the Pinto. Like Mateski probably did the Bonneville.

Should I follow him?

Very unlikely that Farrell would try anything tonight. He would want to get settled in, do some minor surveillance of Vale on his own, get comfortable with the information Mateski had shared, tool around town a little and get the lay of the land. And I didn't mean Snapper Jenny.

I felt confident I'd be easily able to track Farrell down. He'd be at one of Stockwell's half a dozen active motels—there were two resorts and another half dozen motels shuttered for the season—and I should be able to do that yet tonight. Then I would stake him out, watch for my opportunity, and if necessary follow him to Vale's studio and intervene there. That Farrell would not have a quick kill in mind was helpful, as he'd probably be grabbing the dance instructor and transporting him somewhere for a road company show of *The Marquis De Sade Follies*. Too bad there wasn't a poster for Vale to frame.

Farrell could wait.

Right now I needed to handle Mateski. I glanced at him in the mirror, still seated back there in his booth. He wouldn't leave immediately after Farrell, that was a lock. At the moment he was talking to his waitress. She was a cute blonde, a little broad in the beam, thirties, probably a single working mom. Was he ordering more food? No. He was hitting on her!

He had just asked her out. I knew this because I had rudimentary lip-reading skills developed on surveillance stints over the years. These skills hadn't helped with Farrell because he'd said very little, just sitting listening to Mateski, whose back had been to me. But now Mateski was turned toward the waitress, which aimed his face toward the barroom mirror. *What time do you get off work, beautiful?* Ah, Mateski, you smooth son of a bitch....

She let him down gently—my view of her was a sideways one, which is tricky to read, but I think she said, *Sorry, honey, I have an early morning tomorrow.* Maybe the truth. Working mom.

Sunday night was lousy for scoring a pick-up at the Spike. This I knew despite my own luck outside by the garbage cans. Friday and Saturday, and even some weeknights, it wouldn't be that tough. This was the kind of almost upscale shitkicker bar that doubled as a meat market.

But I didn't figure the chunky redheaded antiques dealer would get anywhere, though striking out with the waitress hadn't been enough to dissuade him. Two foxy-looking twenty-something gals down the bar, in jeans and bandana halter tops and lots of permed hair, were deep in a conversation that Mateski, climbing onto a stool next to one of them, tried to enter casually. They weren't having any, and he wasn't getting any.

Those two might have been up for it with the right couple of guys, particularly in their own age group. But Mateski was no John Travolta, and the girls weren't into antiques.

His eyes caught mine in the mirror, and I thought this might turn into a bad moment, but he just gave me a fraternal shrug, and I shrugged back at him, as if to say, *You're right—can't blame a guy for tryin'.*

He had already settled up with the waitress who'd turned him down, and now he went back over to the booth, got glumly into his quilted ski jacket, and trundled out.

I hung back five minutes, so it wouldn't be obvious. Settled my two-buck tab with a keep-the-change five-spot, leaving Mary Ann on good if not promising terms. Then I ambled out into the cold, yawning, glancing around the parking lot, looking casual but in fact alert, gripping the nine millimeter in my jacket pocket.

If I'd been made by Jenny—or if Mateski had noticed me in that bar as a guy he'd seen around town a few too many times to be safe—I could have a king-size problem on my hands. The last thing I needed was to have some asshole who specialized in torture decide to question me about what the fuck I thought I was doing here in Stockwell.

But nobody accosted me, and I got into the Pinto and headed in the direction I figured Mateski had gone—he would either go back to the Rest Haven Court for one last night, or right on by out to Highway 218.

When I passed the motel, no car was parked at Cabin 12. That didn't surprise me. The way the Bonneville was loaded up with primitive paintings and other horseshit, I didn't figure another night there was in the cards. So Highway 218 it was.

And it took only ten minutes to catch up with him. I'd had to push the Pinto's meager horsepower to do so, and even then I didn't want to go over the speed limit—getting stopped by a cop was not a good idea, not with the nine mil in my jacket.

But I counted on Mateski having stopped at a gas station to

fuel up before his trip home, and to maybe grab some snacks and a restroom break. That should make up for the five minutes I'd purposely lagged behind at the Spike. Apparently my thinking was correct, because there up ahead was the Bonneville's big ass with Mateski's big ass in it.

Traffic was light, and often I was right behind him, though I tried to keep at least one car between us whenever possible. The Bonneville was doing fifty-five and so was the Pinto, but my mind was racing.

Should I stay on him?

Did I need to remove him, at the next gas station, or when he pulled in at some motel? I didn't think he could make it all the way back to Woodstock on one tank of gas.

Did he need killing?

Whenever I had worked with a passive partner, I requested that my other half hang around town or at least the area, in case I needed back-up. But certain other active hitters preferred sending surveillance guys on their merry way. Mateski and Farrell had made their contact, and would not necessarily be back in touch over the next few days. Probably unlikely they would be.

At some point, assuming I was successful, Mateski would discover the job had gone south—that Farrell was dead. I didn't do accidents, so the antiques dealer would know an interloper had taken his partner out. He would inform his middleman, assuming there was one, and another passive-active pair would be sent out to do the job, and do it *right* this time.

But not immediately. Not for a week or even a month or maybe not at all. That would give me time to find out which of Candy Stockwell's family or friends had hired Vale's killing, and once the person who hired the job was out of the picture, there'd be no incentive for Mateski or his middleman to do anything further.

Or so it seemed to me, as I tailed the Bonneville through a cold dark night on Highway 218, a dreary underlit stretch of Midwestern nothingness enlivened only by the oldies station I was listening to on the car radio.

Songs I had listened to with the girl I wound up marrying right before I went off to Vietnam. Songs that were popular when, a few years later, I came back and found her in bed with some asshole. Even the song that had been playing on the radio when I went over to that asshole's house just to talk to him, but when he smart-mouthed me from under that sportscar he was working on, I kicked out the jack and crushed him to shit and almost went to prison for it, almost, and that had been a big part of the Broker noticing me. Songs like that.

I followed him for sixty-some miles and then pulled into a gas station, got the Pinto's tank filled, and headed back to Stockwell. Had I done the right thing? Hard to know. This profession I had invented for myself was no exact fucking science.

As was proven when I rolled into town, pulled into the Holiday Inn lot, got out, stretched, and glanced across the street at the Rest Haven Court, where a gray Chevy Cavalier, four-door, '80 or '81 model, was parked in front of Cabin 12.

I went up to my room in the Holiday Inn and I sat in the dark by the window looking out across at the Rest Haven and that parked Chevy for probably half an hour, as if it were a mirage that might disappear.

Lights were on in Cabin 12 for the first twenty minutes, then went out. It was midnight and presumably the torturer in there had gone to bed. He'd traveled a good distance today. Probably he was tuckered.

So was I, but tough shit—I had things to do. I had to think this through. What did it mean, Farrell using the same room

Mateski had? That was hardly standard operating procedure. Normally, beyond one meeting, the passive and active halves of a hit team stayed as far apart as possible, wanting to avoid anything that might connect them in anyone's mind.

But after I mulled it a while, the answer came like somebody threw a switch. I smiled. Simple, and actually pretty smart. There had been no exchange of documents tonight, no notes handed over, because that material had been left behind in Cabin 12, by one partner for the other.

Almost certainly Mateski had paid for Cabin 12 in advance, say for two weeks, or however long the team figured the entire job would take. No one at the Rest Haven was apt to notice the switch in inhabitants, and if they did, so what, who cared? The room had been paid for, hadn't it?

The Vale hit would go down soon. Tomorrow most likely, and if not, the following day. Mr. Roger, in separating himself from those in the community who viewed him as a pariah, had indeed made himself a sitting duck in that black bunker. A sitting duck served up on a silver platter.

How best to handle this?

Was there any reason to fear this torturer more than any other professional in the killing business? Probably not. If things went awry, he would just kill me, not torture me to death—after all, no one would be paying him for the fancy stuff.

Still, the idea of taking on a professional killer capable of systematically snipping away your fingers, toes and penis, and doing so in a way that keeps you alive for the longest, most painful, despair-ridden time, was…off-putting.

Precautions were needed. I didn't want to fuss with the noise suppressor—silencers are unwieldy, and if things got to the point of shooting, noise would be the least of my problems. The clothes I had on would do—sweatshirt and jeans—and the sheathed hunting knife clipped onto my belt just fine. I disliked knives, but sometimes they came in handy. From my suitcase, I took the switchblade, five inches long (ten extended) and half an inch wide, with no hilt. Also a small standard screwdriver, which I stuck in my right pants pocket, in case the old motel had doorknobs and I needed to pop a night latch. For night-latched doors with handles, all I needed was a rubber band, and I took a handful of those, loose in the bottom of the suit-case. In the bathroom, I rolled up my right pant leg and shaved my lower leg and then duct-taped the switchblade to my calf, enough tape to secure it, but not so much to require a hard tug.

I took some deep breaths. Got my shit together. Made sure I had a full clip in the nine millimeter. Loaded the .38 snubnose. Slipped into my fleece-lined jacket. Placed the nine mil in the right jacket pocket, snubby in the left. Snapped on surgical gloves.

Just after three A.M., I crossed the Holiday Inn lot. The street could only have looked deader if tumbleweed were rolling down. Not that long ago, the night had been pleasant enough for an outdoor blow job. By the time I'd left the Spike it was chilly. Now it was cold. My breath smoked.

Hands in my jacket pockets gripping guns, I walked over to the Rest Haven Court, to the slightly larger cabin near the neon sign (VACANCY). I looked in the side window nearest the front. A bell was over the door. Okay. Nobody in the small front office, though a light was on. I moved to the side window toward the back. Sheer curtains were drawn, but I could see a bald man in his forties in a plaid shirt asleep in his chair in front of a TV with snow on the screen. The white noise of it bled through the window.

Out front, I carefully opened the door, reaching up to grab and silence the bell. I stepped inside, leaving the door slightly ajar. The small front office had several STOCKWELL: MISSOURI'S LITTLE VACATIONLAND posters on the walls, a small waiting area with chairs and old magazines, and several racks of tourist booklets. The counter had a mini-rack of the vacation fliers, a guest registration book, a ding-type bell for service, and a modern cash register. Through an open doorway, I could see the snowy TV screen and hear the accompanying hiss; I could not see the sleeper facing it, not from this angle.

Anyway, I hoped he was sleeping. I did not care for collateral damage.

When I slipped behind the counter, I could see the guy now, and he was deep asleep, wire-frame glasses having slid down his nose. Snoring, hands folded across a shirt-button-separating paunch. I allowed myself a smile, grabbed the spare key to Cabin 12 off its hook, made sure that bell didn't jangle when I shut the door quietly, and went back out into a night that seemed even colder now.

Breath pluming, I walked the short distance to the row of cabins, then stopped and took stock. Not including Farrell's Chevy, five cars were parked in spaces. No cars outside Cabins 10 and 11. Good. The doors to rooms had handles, not knobs. Even better.

I tried to look in the window of 12, but the curtains were drawn, the fabric heavy, though the slight space between the curtains, and beneath them, gave no indication of any bleed-through of light. No glow from under the door, either. There seemed to be nothing beyond this door but the room, its inhab-itant, and darkness. At the door, I placed my ear and listened for a good minute. Maybe I heard snoring.

Maybe.

Certainly no conversation, no television, no phone talk. It was after three in the morning, wasn't it? Every reason to believe Farrell was sleeping, probably sleeping soundly.

Or was there some way I could be walking into a trap? Was Snapper Jenny not what she seemed? Had I been made somehow? And got suckered into some kind of elaborate set-up?

With the nine mil in my left hand now, my back to the street side, concealing my activity, I inserted the key slowly, turned it, winced at the tiny click, worked the handle, then eased the door slightly open until the chain of the expected night latch stopped me. I paused to see if I got any reaction from within the room.

None. And I could hear a gentle snoring accompanying deep breathing.

From my jacket pocket I removed one rubber band about five inches in length. I was good at this, but there would be some noise—there was always a little chain rattle. It was an entry technique worth a shit only if the occupant was deep asleep or an invalid. My odds here were okay at best. If I got a reaction from within the room, I'd have to shoulder the door open, bursting the night latch and going in shooting. At which point I'd wonder if that fucking noise suppressor might not have been worth taking, after all.

For now, the fingers of my right hand in the surgical glove slipped inside the ajar door and secured the rubber band around the bolt on the chain at the end of the metal track. The hours I'd practiced this trick had paid off before, but right now I really needed to be deft. My fingers felt for the rubber band and stretched it to loop taut around the tip of the door handle. I pulled the door almost shut—another eighth of an inch and I'd have to unlock it again—which slid the rubber band with the chain on its linear track, chain-bolt still connected to the rubber band, which broke with a snap as I pushed the door all the way open. I went in, transferring my nine mil to my right hand.

There had been some noise, and certainly as I shut the door

behind me there was a click. But he appeared still to be deep asleep, a long slender figure under covers, on his back, snoring gently.

Faking?

Buying time, maybe, to reach for that .22 Magnum automatic on the nightstand?

But he was still sleeping when, after sweeping his little automatic onto the floor, I straddled him, sitting on his stomach, my knees pinning his arms, and pressed his big fluffy spare pillow down over his face, pushing hard, making sure his nose and mouth were getting the brunt without putting so much into it that there would be bruising, the nine mil still in my right hand as I bore down, and when he woke up and started flailing, the kicking he did was useless, the can-can of a dying chorus girl.

It took about two minutes that to me seemed much longer— probably true for him, as well, though those two minutes or so could hardly compare to the suffering he'd over the years administered to others.

Hey, I wasn't here to punish him. *He* was the sick fuck, not me.

I just wanted him dead.

FIVE

I had put in for a nine o'clock wake-up call, even though that meant getting only five hours of sleep. But I wanted to be at my window onto the Rest Haven Court around the time housekeeping would start on the cabins. I sat in my shorts and t-shirt and watched, drinking some coffee and chewing on a Danish that Room Service brought me.

Rest Haven housekeeping was a black woman in her forties or fifties with a cart. It occurred to me she was the first non-white I'd seen in Stockwell. Judging by the cars I'd spotted last night, only about half the cabins were taken, and three of the cars at this time of the morning were still in their spaces, including the Chevy Cavalier, of course. That left three rooms for housecleaning at this point, and she started down at number 4. That gave me time to shower and brush my teeth and take a crap. When I returned to the window, she was on the second of the three car-less cabins. So I got up and put on a sweatshirt and jeans.

By ten-thirty she had cleaned the three cabins, and now began again on the cabins with cars parked outside. She would knock, saying something (presumably, *"Housekeeping!"*), and in the first two instances was apparently told to come back later. Last night I'd noticed no DO NOT DISTURB signs, so apparently the Rest Haven Court did not splurge on such niceties.

When she tried the door to Cabin 12, she for some reason didn't get a response from the occupant. She unlocked the door with her passkey and went in. Perhaps a minute and a half later she came out. She looked only mildly upset. Not that I had

expected her to come out screaming, *"Laws a'mighty!"* People
die in their sleep in motel and hotel rooms all the time.

She did move fairly briskly over to the manager's office in the
oversize cabin by the neon sign, leaving her push cart behind,
and I took in the action with the bored semi-interest of somebody watching a *Love Boat* rerun (one of which was playing on
my room's television, volume down low enough to keep me
company but not distract me). The manager came out, moving
quickly, and she followed. This was a small man in a brown suit,
tie flapping, not the bald snoring guy of the night before. She
waited outside as he went in. He came out in under a minute.
He said something to her along the lines of *"You need to wait
here,"* and went back to his office. She lighted up a cigarette
and leaned back against the windows of Cabin 12. White man
dead in bed. Smoke 'em if you got 'em.

I went over and swung the desk-perched TV around to face
me. A lot would happen now over at the Rest Haven, but the
pace might be slow. *The Love Boat* was over. Pretty soon a very
dumb game show on NBC came on, called *Hit Man*. I wouldn't
kid you.

What I was watching for was whether the cabin got treated
like a crime scene. I didn't figure it would, and I was right. A
patrol car with two uniformed cops arrived first, then a Ford
Fairmont driven by a dumpy guy in a dumpy suit pulled in—a
plainclothes cop. He and the manager went into 12 and weren't
gone long. The plainclothes cop was giving the manager instructions and the manager was nodding. Then all the cops left.

During *Family Feud*, an ambulance arrived, no siren, no
hurry. Within five minutes, the body of a man who had caused
so much suffering to so many (you're welcome) was carried out
in a body bag. No need for a gurney for so short a distance.

Not a crime scene, then. No small-town forensics guy, no

photography, no yellow-and-black tape. Some guy had died in his sleep. Because the room had been Mateski's originally, Farrell would probably be listed under whatever fake name his partner checked in under—a good chance that was the name Farrell had used, too, to keep things clean. When the dead man's I.D. would prove to turn up nothing interesting—no priors, no relatives—that Chevy Cavalier would be seized and eventually raffled off for some city or county fund or other.

Was I a genius to predict all this? No, I just knew how deaths in the lodging business were handled, particularly in a small-town vacation destination. No hotel likes its living guests disturbed by the exit of a deceased one. Vacationers get sent the wrong signal when people are dying around them. Even businessmen on the road don't like the thought that they might die in bed, far from home.

So motels and hotels checked dead guests out with as little fanfare and as much alacrity as possible, with (in Stockwell's case, anyway) the cops complicit in helping along the town's main industry. I'd been careful to avoid bruising Farrell and the only thing that might indicate he hadn't died in his sleep of a heart attack or aneurism would be his slightly bloodshot eyes, if anybody bothered to notice. That was a byproduct of forced suffocation.

Anyway, by eleven-thirty the housekeeper was rolling her cart back into Cabin 12. She didn't look at all put out about it. If people have seen enough in their time, they can get pretty hardened, I guess.

I thought about calling Vale to let him know the heat was off, but I didn't want to discuss that kind of thing on the phone. Face-to-face was called for, and I wasn't up to it right now. I was beat, suffused with the kind of tiredness you feel when you've been working hard and the stress had lifted.

So I kicked off my sneakers and flopped onto the bed in my clothes and fell asleep in seconds. No worries about being bothered. The Holiday Inn was a class joint, DO NOT DISTURB hangers and everything.

The dance studio was just a black shape in a late afternoon already turning to night. Cold again, if not as much so as last night, though I'd left my fleece-lined jacket behind, substituting a camel sport jacket; I'd also replaced the sweatshirt and jeans with a light blue long-sleeve shirt and chinos. There was a chance I would run into parents at the studio, dropping their girls off for private lessons. From here on out, on my Stockwell sojourn, I was a journalist, and needed to class my look up a tad.

Vale was expecting me. I had called from a pay phone and said I needed to stop over—was five-thirty all right? He'd said his lessons started at seven, and I said this shouldn't take long. Could he have my five grand handy?

The slender dance instructor let me in the front door after I knocked and identified myself. His handsome, narrow, hooded-eyed features had an apprehensive aspect, probably because I'd jumped him the last time he'd answered my knock at these doors.

I smiled easily, said, "Everything's cool. Nothing to worry about."

A white grin flashed under the Tom Selleck mustache, in the orange-tinged tanned face, and he sighed in an almost comic weight-of-the-world manner. "Good to hear, good to hear."

He was back in his black tee, tights and Capezios. As he led me into the half of his quarters where we'd spoken before, he gestured toward the kitchenette. Some rye bread and cold cuts and cheese slices were on a plate on the counter.

"I was just getting ready to fix myself a sandwich," he said. "Can I make you one?"

"No thanks. Why don't we sit down? You might not want to be eating when I make my report."

Following my assurance that everything was cool, this threw him a little. I meant it to.

"Oh," he said. "Okay."

We sat as before, me on the brown-leather couch under the framed Broadway posters, him on the edge of the nearby matching comfy chair.

"The man sent to kill you is out of the picture," I said.

"By which you mean...?"

"I'm going to spare you the details. You don't need to know any more than that."

He swallowed. Smoothed his mustache with a thumbnail. He seemed to be trying to decide whether to be relieved or unnerved, and settled for a bit of both. "I can't know who it is *was*, or...?"

"Less you know the better."

He thought about that, brow furrowed. "You said there were... were *two* of them."

"Yeah. The guy watching you, the last week or so? He left town yesterday, after his partner arrived."

"Oh."

I nodded. "They exchanged information, in a public place actually, and the surveillance man headed home. I followed him long enough to make sure."

He was frowning again, confused. "You...you indicated you would have to remove *both* of them."

"I know. And I may still have to. He's a loose end and loose ends sometimes need tying off. But I didn't want to leave the more dangerous half of the team out of my sight for long. And, Roger, that guy was *very* goddamn dangerous."

He swallowed like a kid in the middle of getting the facts of life from his father. "Really?"

"Yeah. You got a bargain at ten grand. If I'd have known who was being sent after you, I'd have either asked for a shit-pot more or taken a pass."

The dark eyes flared. "And just let me *die*?"

"Roger, we're not friends. I didn't know who the fuck you were two weeks ago."

He swallowed again, nodded. "What *made* him so...so dangerous? Or don't you want to talk about it?"

"Actually, we need to talk about that. A bit, anyway. This was a specialist, not just somebody who removed problems. Somebody who made his subjects suffer."

"Subjects?"

"Targets. Victims. You."

He was trembling. "You're trying to scare me again, like you did Sunday. Why are you always trying to scare me?"

"I'm not trying to scare you, Roger, and anyway, you *should* be scared because somebody obviously wants you more than just dead."

That seemed to knock him back. "What's '*more* than just *dead*'?"

"I told you. Pay attention. Whoever hired this done wanted you to suffer before you died." I sighed. "Roger, the man sent to kill you had a reputation in my business. A reputation for torturing people. To death. Slowly."

"That's...that's *crazy*. Why would anyone want that?"

"For revenge." I shrugged. "Somebody thinks you murdered Candy Stockwell, and they loved her so much that *that's* how much they hate you."

"What do you mean, exactly...torture?"

I gave him some examples.

"Jesus Christ," he gasped.

"Actually, he *did* crucify a guy once. Priest who diddled a choir boy who was a mobster's nephew."

He rushed over to the sink and puked. I waited while he

splashed his face with water; finally he staggered over, an extremely awkward gait for a guy in Capezios.

As he sat down, leaning back this time, he was trembling even more visibly. His face was white, or as white as the phony tan would allow.

His voice seemed distant as he asked, "Why should I believe you?"

"What do you mean?"

"How do I know this isn't some sort of shakedown? Maybe you're a cop. Maybe you're...what do they call it? Wearing a wire! And you're trying to get me to confess to something I didn't do."

"Aw, shit," I said.

I stood, took off the sport jacket, tossed it on the couch. Unbuttoned the long-sleeve shirt, slipped it off, tossed it on the jacket, did a pirouette that was unlikely to get me a slot in his dance class.

Then I spread my hands and said, "Satisfied?"

He nodded a bunch of times and I put myself back together. "It's not a shakedown."

"Well, you can see why I might think it is."

I sat down. "No. I can't."

Again he sat forward, his expression painfully earnest. "Quarry, you come around a week and a half ago, you say somebody has hired a contract on me. You come around later and wave a gun around and scare me some more. Now you show up and you say you've killed the killer, but can't tell me who it was because the less I know the better off I am, and can you have your other five grand, please?"

Maybe he had a point.

I sighed. I pointed toward the phone on the wall in the kitchenette area. "Go call the Rest Haven Court."

He frowned in confusion. "What? That sleazy motel across from the Holiday Inn?"

"That's the one. Tell them you're…what's the name of the local paper?"

"The *Sentinel*."

"Tell them you're calling from the *Sentinel* and wondered if the guest who died in Cabin Twelve had been identified yet. Ask if they can provide any details at all."

He thought about that for a moment, then nodded, and went over quickly. He got a phone book from somewhere, found and called the number, and did as I asked. He listened to the answers, then said goodbye, hung up, and returned to the comfy chair.

"Well?" I asked.

"They said the name of the guest who died is being withheld till the family can be notified, but that it was death by natural causes. He died in his sleep due to a heart attack."

Pretty specific, considering I doubted anybody had done an autopsy.

"And," Vale went on, "I was advised to check with the police before putting anything about it in the paper."

"No surprise."

"…*You* did that?"

"Yes."

He sat forward again, eyes tensed. "You *really* did that? How? With a needle, or…?"

"You don't fucking need to know."

That had come across a little stern, and he seemed almost hurt as he defensively asked, "Well, what about that *other* man? The surveillance one? You seem awfully vague about it. Content to let him roam around and maybe team up with some other torturer. Vlad the Impaler possibly. Torquemada maybe."

"I'm pretty sure those guys are dead, Roger."

"Very droll I'm sure."

I sat forward. "Look, I don't take taking lives lightly. We're lucky that the police here look the other way when a motel

guest croaks and disrupts the tourist industry. You'd think in
the off-season they might take it more seriously, but no.
Anyway, there won't *be* a second team of professionals killer
sent to remove you—not if we act now."

He nodded slowly. "You mean, if I give you the go-ahead to
find out who did this?"

"Right. But you need to decide, and decide now. I may only
have a few days to pull this off."

"How…how would you do it?"

I gestured to my spiffed-up look. "As far as anyone in Stockwell is concerned, I'm a reporter for the *St. Louis Sun*. That
allows me to go around asking questions. I'll talk to everybody
you consider capable of paying to have you killed. Particularly
those you consider capable of wanting the kind of sadistic
revenge we're talking about. And I'll assess the situation. That
simple."

His eyes were wide. "Simple. And you'll kill *that* person, too?
If it's one of the Stockwells, and it almost *has* to be, that's not
some anonymous out-of-towner dying 'in his sleep' in a motel
room. Say it's the old man. He's feared and revered in this town.
That's as front-page a death as you could find in this part of the
state. How would you manage it? And don't tell I don't need to
know. I'll still be living here, and I'll be the prime suspect!"

"Good point. We'll make sure you have an alibi when I take
that step."

"But *how* will you take it?"

I shrugged. "Probably with a bullet. I don't stage fake accidents—that's a specialty, like torture. But I can rig a suicide or
a robbery. We'll be fine."

He laughed without humor. "And this will be another ten
thousand?"

"That's what I quoted you, yes. I'll stand by that. And you
don't have to pay me a dollar till the job's done."

That sent his eyebrows up and his attitude shifted. "Really? Why is that?"

"Frankly, I can't guarantee I can pull off this part of the assignment. I can only spend a few days at it, before getting rid of the guy in Cabin Twelve catches up with me."

"Because you didn't deal with the surveillance guy, you mean."

I shook my head. "Even if I had, the middleman who sent them will know very soon that they failed."

"Middleman…?"

I nodded. "There was almost certainly a middleman involved, someone with mob ties probably, hired by whoever it is locally that wants you taken out, literally in the worst way."

He was thinking. "So if whoever hired this is *dead*, then the contract goes away…?"

"Right. When we first talked, you said you could afford the fee. Despite you puking in the sink, Roger, I do think you have the stomach for this. Do I go home now, and leave you to take your chances…or do I take a swing at finding and removing your local problem?"

He nodded, once. No hesitation. "Do it."

I smiled. "Okay, then. Got that five grand handy?"

More nods as he got up and went over to his rolltop and retrieved a fat envelope from a cubbyhole. He brought it over and handed it to me, sat again. I didn't insult him by counting it, just stuffed it away in my sport jacket.

"Any other questions?" I asked.

He shook his head. He sank back into the chair. He wasn't small but he wasn't big, either, and seemed to be swallowed up in it. He looked like a guy in the midst of a bad bout of flu.

"You all right, Roger?"

"I don't know. I'm hoping I will be, when this is over. For months now, I've been a prisoner in my own castle. You have any idea what that's like?"

I did. I'd been holed up before with people out there looking to kill me. That happened sometimes.

But I said, "No. Must be rough."

He swallowed. His voice had a quaver. "I'm just trying to stand up for my reputation, in the face of one of the most powerful, ruthless families in the Midwest. I mean, they tried to get the police to put me away, and they slandered me, and now they are trying to *kill* me."

"It's a bitch," I said.

He leaned forward. The dark eyes were moist. "Do you have any idea what it's like to be a gay man in a backward community like this? Before this Candy Stockwell debacle, I could maintain a relationship in a nearby community. Discreetly, but I could have somebody in my life. Since this…this *siege* began, I've been trapped here. The person I was seeing dropped me like a hot potato. Do you know what it's like not to be in a serious relationship? To be alone?"

Actually, I did, and I didn't mind. Not as long as there were waitresses in Geneva, Wisconsin, who liked to spend the occasional evening on Paradise Lake.

"I…I know I doubted you. And I'm sorry, Quarry. Genuinely sorry. You came here to help me and I appreciate that. I really do. To a man bouncing off the walls, you're a goddamn savior!"

"It's what I do."

He leaned forward and put a hand on my knee. "I really appreciate it. Believe me. I hope you understand that—"

I lifted his hand off my leg like a leaf that had drifted there from an autumn tree.

"Roger, I got nothing against homosexuals," I said. "Who sticks what in whose what's-it is none of my concern. I worked side-by-side with a gay guy for years, no problem. He was a good man. But if you put your hand my leg again, *we're* gonna have a problem."

"Understood," he said, and sat back. "Apologies."

"None needed."

"A man gets lonely."

"I hear you."

Somebody was coming in the front door. I reached for the little automatic in my jacket pocket—I had helped myself to Farrell's .22 Mag—but Roger patted the air with a palm.

"That will be Sally," he said. "She always gets here at least half an hour before my first lesson. She assists me in everything."

I nodded. "She's got a huge crush on you, you know."

He waved that off as he stood. "No, it's more a dad-and-daughter thing…she lost both her folks in an automobile accident, several years ago, lives with her aunt….Wait here a sec."

He went out and I put the .22 away.

Soon Sally—in her white fur coat—strode in with Roger right behind her, her big head of frizzy tawny-blonde hair like a halo gotten out of hand.

She draped the fur coat over the rolltop's chair; her curvy little body was decked out in an off-the-shoulders violet mini-dress with white bunnies running around the wide collarless collar, with a white belt and purple tights and matching violet leg warmers above lighter violet lace-up shoes.

Roger asked, "You want something to drink, sweetie?"

"I'll get myself a Diet Coke," she said. Looking my way, she asked, "Anybody else?"

"No thanks," I said.

Roger came over and leaned before me with his hands on his knees and said, sotto voce, "You and Sally are going to be *great* friends."

Really?

Roger stage-directed her over to the couch, where she nestled beside me. Not close, but not far—I could easily smell her

Charlie perfume from here. She sat sipping Diet Coke with her violet knees primly together. She was very cute, if you liked jailbait. And what man doesn't, really?

Roger sat on the edge of the chair. He was going just a little bit into his swishy mode. "Sweetie, this is Jack. Jack Quarry, a good friend of mine from St. Louis."

"Hi, Jack," she said noncommittally, not looking at me.

"Hi," I said.

"Honey, Jack is helping me with this terrible fix I'm in. He's writing a story for a newspaper all about how I've been persecuted over your friend's disappearance.…Jack, Sally was Candy's best friend."

"Really," I said.

"I was," she said. "I *am.*" Suddenly she was gazing guilelessly at me with big baby-blue eyes, the color of her Mustang. Nothing wary there now. "If there's anything you want to know about Candy, I'm your girl."

Roger said, "Sally, there may be some people Jack wants to talk to, *needs* to talk to, who you could pave the way with. Teachers, for example. Some of her other friends, perhaps."

Sally frowned in thought. Looking at her closely, I could see she was an older teen all right, but her features were a child's. A pretty child's.

"There's a parent–teacher night tomorrow," she said. "I don't have anybody to go with me, and maybe Mr. Quarry could take me. I could say he was my uncle or something."

Roger turned to me brightly. "How does that sound, Jack?"

"Sounds pretty good."

She asked, "Would you like my phone number?"

Was she kidding?

SIX

So now I had two phone numbers from two attractive females here in the Little Vacationland of Missouri (off-season). One was a petite tawny-blonde cheerleader who was maybe legal— Sally's last name was Meadows, by the way, with all its running-barefoot-through connotations—but I didn't need to call her, because we already had a date for the Parent–Teacher Night at the high school tomorrow. Next stop, Junior/Senior Prom.

The other was the black sheep (or was that ewe?) of the Stockwell family. Like a '77 Camaro, Jenny had some miles on her, but plenty of pick-up. Her phone number remained faintly visible on my left wrist despite efforts to wash it off.

From my Holiday Inn room, I gave her a call—it was a quarter to seven.

"Hello," the husky voice answered.

"Sounds like Jenny."

"It is Jenny. Do I know you?"

"Jack from the Spike last night. Remember me?"

"Remember you? Hell, I can still taste you."

That made me laugh and my dick gave a little nod at my good sense to call this woman. "I was wondering if you might like to go out for a drink."

"I haven't eaten yet, Jack. You want to do something about that?"

"Sure. But I don't know my way around this vacation wonderland. What would you suggest?"

Tony's Italiano was downtown, a block over from Antiques Row, a long narrow affair with pine booths on one side and tables everywhere else, kitchen in back. No bar, and nothing fancy—the wall mural of Italian gardens with marble statues was as cheesy as anything on the menu, and the red-and-white checkered tablecloths were plastic. But the garlic-tinged fragrance of marinara was inviting enough.

Jenny Stockwell was sitting in the farthest back booth and I had to walk damn near the length of the place to find her. I almost didn't recognize her. Not that the basic biker girl look was entirely gone, just amped up into Pat Benatar territory. Her silver-streaked black gypsy curls went fine with the black vinyl shoulder-pads-and-zipper jacket worn over a black mini and dark nylons, set off by red cuffs and a wide red belt.

I was still in the sport jacket ensemble I'd worn to Vale's, if you're interested. Nicer than last night, but outclassed by Jenny Stockwell, whose money was showing.

I slid in across from her. "Hope you haven't been waiting long."

"Just long enough to order us a bottle of Chablis. I know you're supposed to drink red wine with Italian food, but that shit gives me a headache."

I said white wine was fine with me, told her she looked fantastic, and made small talk waiting for, and during, the meal.

She did not work, she said—she was living off family money, not a bit ashamed of it, and was trying to be a novelist. She was in a local writers' group consisting of other women in their thirties and forties hoping to break into the romance market. "Isn't just hearts and flowers, Jack, not anymore—it's steamy as hell. Porn for chicks."

It occurred to me that maybe her bar crawling was research for sex scenes, but I didn't express the thought. She'd not sold anything yet, though had come close, and even had an agent interested.

Jenny had been married and divorced three times. She had a

child, a boy, by the first husband, a truck driver who had tried
to get alimony and custody, and got neither. Her son, David,
was a freshman at the University of Missouri now, a good kid
making his grandfather proud, though she and her son always
had "a strained relationship."

"David never liked my lifestyle," she said, with a shrug. "He
was ashamed of me. If I didn't love the little bastard...." She
sighed. "He divorced me, like the other men in my life."

"What do you mean?"

"In junior high, he divorced me. Kids can do that, you know,
and his grandfather gave him the legal help to do it. I was a 'bad
influence,' and an alcoholic. I may be a free spirit, Jack, but I'm
no goddamn fucking alcoholic."

She was on her third glass of Chablis.

"We have a sort of truce these days," she said. "I think as he
gets older, David may come to accept me on my own terms.
You know, he broke my heart when he divorced me, and moved
in with his grandparents. They turned him into another Mr.
Plastic Conservative Businessman like the other Stockwell men."

"How old was David when he left you?"

"Twelve."

I sipped my Coke. "No other kids?"

No. Some "mishap" in her second pregnancy had left her
unable to conceive, and the other two husbands were apparently after her money but didn't get anywhere ("a punk and a
drunk," respectively). She'd lived with a couple of guys since,
but these days men were mostly just a "recreational pursuit" to
her, "a hobby, not a job."

The above isn't meant to suggest she was so self-centered as
to not inquire about my background. She did. I gave her a trun-
cated version of my real life story—Midwestern boy, Vietnam,
cheating wife—but substituted journalism for killing.

We had tiramisu, one plate, two spoons, very intimate for a first date, although last night's blow job perhaps qualified this as the second date.

We were having coffee when I said, "You know, kind of surprises me to learn you're a writer."

"Why's that, Jack? Don't you think I've had enough stimulating life experiences to draw upon?"

"I would think you have. But when I mentioned I was in town to write about the local arts scene, you didn't seem at all interested."

"The local art scene bores the shit out of me."

"Ah."

"But I've always been involved in the arts. Lit major in college, wanted to be a poet, figured I was the female Rod McKuen. Lived with a guitar player for a while and we used to play some coffee houses and clubs around Missouri and Illinois—my Carole King singer-songwriter phase. Painted for a while. A gallery in town was selling some of my stuff, but I got frustrated."

"Why's that?"

"The only thing people were buying was the self-portrait nudes. That's flattering in a way, but also insulting. A girl likes to think she's more than just tits and ass."

Jenny, attractive though she was, had not been a "girl" for some time. She was clearly zeroing in on forty, and that reading was based on flattering low lighting.

Still, she was a striking woman whatever her age, that wide red mouth with the lipstick less extreme tonight, the same for the mascara aiding those green translucent eyes that needed no help at all.

"The story I gave you last night," I said, "about the local arts—that was actually bullshit."

Her eyebrows went up but she was not astonished. It was

just possible she'd been lied to by a man in a bar before. "So you're not a reporter?"

"I *am* a freelance journalist, and I'm doing a story, but the arts aspect of it is tangential."

She grinned. "'Tangential'? You *are* a writer, aren't you, Jack?"

"Well, you are too, so I figured you could keep up."

She lighted a Camel, eyeing me appraisingly. "So what *are* you writing about? Doing an exposé on the activities of middle-aged women who pick up strange men in dives?"

"The Spike *is* kind of a dive, but I'm not that strange, and I wouldn't call you middle-aged."

She blew out a blue cloud. "Most of the tail I'm up against in those meat markets is around half my age. You know what they say, Jack—when you're number two, you gotta try harder."

I sipped my coffee. "You consider these young single girls your competition?"

"Damn straight."

"What are you competing for? Aren't three sour marriages enough? You still looking for Prince Charming? Look what happened to Diane Keaton when she went looking for Mr. Right."

"That was Mr. Goodbar, wasn't it?" She shivered. "Depressing damn movie. So…what's your article about, Jack? Poor little rich girls who refuse to grow up?"

"You're under the false impression that this song is about you. You may be part of it, but that's a coincidence. I honestly didn't know you were a Stockwell."

Her eyes narrowed, and as she listened to what I next had to say, her flip manner faded.

"What I'm really writing about is the disappearance of your niece—Candy. My understanding is that certain members of your family believe this local dance instructor, Roger Vale, is responsible somehow. They made public accusations that he may have kidnapped and murdered your niece, and yet Vale has never sued."

"All right." Her voice had changed. Husky as ever, but all the humor was out. No anger, though, and the eyes had a new alert hardness. "Let's back this up. You need to convince me you didn't come looking for me. That this really *is* a coincidence."

"Okay…"

"I don't like being used. I may be easy…but I do not fucking like being used."

"Last night? I was sitting at the bar. You came up and sat next to me."

"Okay. And you were sitting at the bar when I came in. Could you have known I'd be there?" Who was she asking, herself or me?

I said, "Is the Golden Spike the only bar in Stockwell you frequent?"

"What do you think?"

"I'm gonna say no. Do you regularly go to the Spike on Sunday night? And is that something I could know?"

She thought about that through a few drags on the Camel. Finally she shook her head, gypsy curls bouncing, then asked, "Nobody pointed me out to you?"

"When you went to the little girl's room, that barmaid told me who you were. But you and I, we'd already struck up a conversation. In fact, you spoke first. Said I had a nice face, remember?"

She smiled. Nodded. "It's still pretty nice."

"Well, you have had three glasses of wine. How about it? Will you help me?"

"How?"

"For starters, tell me about Candy."

She glanced around. No one seemed to be paying any attention to us, but the place was fairly full. She said, "Not here.
Let's go to my place."

I said fine, and paid the bill, even if Jenny Stockwell was
richer than hell. Call it an investment. This might be my first
step on the road to marrying an heiress....

She drove a flashy black Firebird that looked like Robin the
Boy Wonder should've been in the seat next to her. I followed
her through town in my pathetic Pinto as she routinely did
forty, seemingly unconcerned about cops or that I might lose
her. But the moon was full and helped me stay with her, even
when—in a wooded area barely within city limits—she took a
sudden turn off onto an ungated lane marked PRIVATE — NO
TRESPASSING.

The strip of asphalt cut through half a mile of dense trees
and brush. At the end, on a stone-and-pebble hillock, sat a
ranch-style house of stained-amber wood siding, an L-shape,
like two boxcars had jackknifed off the tracks. A one-and-a-half
story tower joined the two wings; the roofs were black and
pitched, but for the backward slant of the tower, creating a geo-
metric effect. Door-sized vertical windows were frequent,
adding to the feeling of nature meeting modernity.

A cement drive led to a two-car garage at the left tip of the L.
She put the Firebird away next to a couple of Harleys and the
door closed automatically. I left the Pinto in the drive and, a kid
crossing a pond, hopped the irregular stone slabs that served as
a sidewalk. Pots for plants were placed here and there, emptied
in anticipation of winter.

The front door opened and she motioned me into a high-
ceilinged entryway, where she took my coat to deposit in a
sliding-door closet, saying, "Let's go into the living room." Her
black vinyl jacket had disappeared—she was just in the black

mini with red belt. She turned on some subdued track lighting, and I got a look at a big room that filled most of this wing, though I'd noticed a modern kitchen coming in, behind me now.

She did have money.

So said the vaulted ceiling and the endless expanse of oak paneling; the walls were off-white plaster spotted with unframed canvases signed JS, primitive paintings Mateski might dig, only these had a real flair—landscapes based on the woodsy view out a wall of windows, marked by a striking, startling use of color, like the inside of a maniac's brain, only better organized.

The furnishings were modular and right out of a rich college kid's apartment—tweed-covered cushions of either off-white or dark brown on chrome-plated steel frames. A group of white cushions formed a couch facing a big tan brick fireplace, two brown ones served as armchairs with matching ottomans. End tables and coffee tables were low-slung and glass-topped.

The fireplace wall bore signs from the Stockwell family's fortune-making but long-dead business—STOCKWELL BRAND BUGGY WHIPS—LIGHT, STURDY, DEPENDABLE—with silhouette of horse and buggy and a driver poised to flick the product; the most modern-looking advertisement (1920?) said STOCKWELL BUGGY WHIPS—TRUE HORSEPOWER. Over the fireplace, on nails, hung four vintage buggy whips. And off to one side, in an antique gilt frame, a Civil War-era funky-sideburned gent posed with a whip in his hands like a ringmaster getting ready to discourage some animal.

"So you do have some family pride," I said.

"Or maybe I just like whips." She gestured to the tweed-cushion-and-chrome couch. "Get comfy. How about something stronger than Coke?"

"Any kind of beer."

"Coors okay?"

"Fine."

She brought me one and sat beside me. She appeared to have made herself a Jack and Ginger.

"You'd be surprised," she said, "how rarely I have a man out to my house."

"Would I?"

"I'm strictly a parking lot and motel brand of slut."

"I don't think you're a slut."

"No?"

"No."

And I didn't. I thought she was one fucked-up dangerous damn piece of ass. Slut didn't quite cover it.

"Well," she said, "whatever I am, I value my privacy. You're a rare guest out here."

"I'm flattered."

She got up and got a fire going. It was gas, so that didn't take long; even so, watching her bend over was a pleasure, legs long and muscular in a sinewy way. Then she went over and turned off the track lighting, the room infused with a nice orange glow as she sat beside me.

She played with my hair absently. "Why should I talk to you about Candy?"

"Because you're her aunt. It's obvious you two were close. Do you think she's still alive?"

"I hope so."

"You don't believe Vale was responsible for whatever happened to her?"

She frowned, sighed, sipped her drink. "He might be, but not the way my father and brother think."

"Explain."

"I don't know Roger Vale that well. I talked to him two or three times, at recitals where Candy was dancing. She was his star pupil. Wonderful dancer. Jazz, not ballet. Sexy child, I mean, my God. Your eyes would've popped out of your head, Jack. No flying shit."

"How could Vale be to blame for her disappearance?"

A shrug. She looked beautiful in the firelight, the shadows doing interesting things to the sharp planes of her face. "I suppose it's possible he had an affair with her. Candy was pretty wild. And I wasn't convinced he was the queen he seemed to be. Might've been bi, might even've been straight, playing up to these hicks. So they'll trust their daughters to him."

"So he can get close to them, you mean? And do what? Have his way with his budding pupils?"

She shook her head; you could almost hear the gypsy thumb cymbals. "No, I don't read it that way. I think he wanted to work closely with the girls, and he's apparently really quite gifted—he had considerable success last year helping some of our girls do well on the pageant circuit."

"I heard. A lot of parents have stood by him."

She nodded. "I know Candy was crazy about him...not romantically, but because he had helped her improve, and was encouraging her to take dance and theater, in college. Even urged her to consider going professional someday. She could sing well, too, you know. And act. Real triple threat. Vale said she had the makings of another Liza Minnelli."

"What do you think?"

"I think he was right. This coming year, after working with Vale, Candy would have killed at the Miss Teen Missouri pageant."

"Then what makes you say he might be responsible for her going missing?"

"He probably wasn't. Not directly. Indirectly? Maybe." She gathered her thoughts, sipping the Jack and Ginger to help her along. "Candy's father...my *brother*, Lawrence...did not approve of Roger Vale encouraging these show business dreams of hers. Larry had told her that entering Miss Teen Missouri was out of the question. Not dignified enough for a Stockwell, and taking theater and dance at college as her major, that was not an option, either."

"Why not?"

She sighed. "Well, we're running out of Stockwells. There was Larry's Candy and my David, and that was it for the next generation. You knew, didn't you, that the heir apparent, Steven, died in Vietnam?"

"No. First I heard."

She shook her head wearily. "In the final months of that fucking war. Nice guy, Steven, though very establishment, very conservative, like his folks and his grandparents."

"I don't get it. A guy from a rich family didn't have to go to Vietnam. That's why God made college deferments."

A dark eyebrow arched. "Not after Uncle Sam trumped God with the draft lottery. Steven drew a low number, something like fourteen, and that put him on the fast track to the Ho Chi Minh Trail. My father tried to pull some strings, but before Dad had managed anything, Steven enlisted in the Marines. And for all their misgivings, our parents were proud of Steven. He won some medals. Made lieutenant."

Plus got his ass killed. Great goddamn war. Where would I be without it?

She was saying, "Steven's death accelerated a drinking problem my mother already had...she died ten years ago, liver failure. Shattered Daddy. Crushed David, living with his grandparents. And then, six, seven years ago? Larry lost Candy's mother Karen to breast cancer, and Jesus, for a while there, it was just the Stockwell family apocalypse."

Rich people had their problems, too. Ask the Kennedys.

"That," she was saying, after a Jack and Ginger booster, "was when Larry started spoiling Candy. Letting her wrap him around her pretty pinkie, buying her everything and anything, fancy cars, expensive clothes. She stayed out to all hours, drugs, drinking, fucking. That's what losing a mom can do to an impressionable young girl. I tried to do what I could—we were very close. But it just didn't any good."

You don't suppose having Aunt Jenny as a role model had anything to do with Candy's wild behavior? I pose this question to you, because I sure as hell wasn't going to bring it up with Aunt Jenny.

Instead, I said, "Doesn't sound like Daddy was 'spoiling' her where her Broadway dreams were concerned."

"No. He wanted her to pursue Steven's dream—a new generation of Stockwell business! Somehow my brother deluded himself into imagining Candy with an MBA, taking over one of the family firms, maybe, or marrying somebody who could."

She let out a short, humorless laugh, then had another swig of Jack and Ginger.

Her smile was bitterly ironic as she continued: "I can just see it—Larry forbidding her to enter the Miss Teen Missouri pageant, Candy flipping out and running off. *That's* why I say she may still be alive."

"You really think so?"

She nodded emphatically. "Candy could be a runaway, Jack. She may be living somewhere, under an assumed name, working as a waitress or something, and trying to break into show business. Hollywood, New York, Toronto, who knows?"

Would a spoiled brat want to work that hard? Yet a girl as cute and talented as Candy *could* be working on some lower show biz rung. Or she might have found a sugar daddy. Possibilities, but they didn't resonate for me.

"So," she said, sitting cozily closer, "how do you think writing an article about all this will do anybody any good?"

"It'll call attention to the case. If I do a good enough job, the piece will get some national play, with Candy's picture splashed around. And if she's alive, somebody will let us know."

"And if she isn't?"

"Well, I intend to explore the possibility of Vale's culpability. Look into why some Stockwell family members consider him a prime suspect in what they feel is Candy's murder."

"And what good will *that* do?"

"Attracting attention to an unsolved crime can have a very positive effect. It might spark the FBI to get involved. Or the Missouri state police, anyway."

She had started nodding halfway through that. She sipped more Jack and Ginger. "How can I help?"

"I was hoping you could pave the way for me with your brother and your father. I need to interview them. But it sounds like you and they might not be on the best of terms."

"No, we're okay. I'm not their favorite, but…I'm about all that's left, except for my son. They know I've been pretty upset since Candy disappeared. They know how much I love her. And with my David coming of age, their *heir apparent*…especially since he and I are getting along marginally better now…they're trying to take me back into the fold, a little. No, I can help you with that."

"Tomorrow maybe? During the day?"

"Sure, Jack. Why not?" She sounded sleepy.

"It's getting late," I said, taking the cue. "I should probably go. What time tomorrow, do you think?"

She kissed me and stuck her tongue in my mouth; it tasted like Jack and Ginger, not surprisingly. And her breath smelled of tobacco. Should have been disgusting. It wasn't.

She slipped out of my arms and stood with her back to the fire, which outlined her in an orange glow, making a near silhouette of her as she undid and threw off the red belt and then pulled the black mini up over her head. She wore nothing beneath. The breasts were large, too perfect, clearly the work of some plastic surgeon, and I did not give a good goddamn, because they were mesmerizing as she swayed before me, dancing to some sensual tune in her head, her pubic thatch an echo of her gypsy hair.

Her figure didn't look bony at all, not in the semi-dark anyway, and when in her dance she turned toward the flames and swayed her dimpled rump at me, I pulled her down on my lap and she giggled and said, "I'll sit on you, front ways. I like that better. Need me to get you a rubber?"

She may have been promiscuous, but she wasn't a fool.

"I got one." I was getting my billfold out.

"Let me put it on for you."

She took the little package, opened it with her teeth. Knelt before me, undid my belt, pulled my shorts and pants down around my ankles, and then lubricated me with her mouth before her lips expertly rolled the condom down over me. Then she sat facing me on my lap with me up inside her and she moved so rhythmically, I started hearing the music, too. Her passion was contagious and made me drunk with her, and for that small piece of time I felt she loved me, her hands caressing my shoulders, my back, mouth hungrily descending on mine, then moving to my neck, to an ear, moaning, groaning, emanating not just heat but warmth. My hands were full of her rounded ass and my mouth was suckling the hard tip of a swollen breast and my nostrils twitched with the nasty sweet scent of her, and when I came, I jerked as helplessly as a cowboy on a bronc, even if I was the one being ridden.

When we slowed to a stop, she put a hand in my hair and played there. She smiled at me so tenderly that all the barroom hardness disappeared. "Stay the night, Jack, why don't you?"

"Okay," I said.

SEVEN

On either side of the double doors of the two-story brown-red brick building with green terra cotta trim, a bronze lion on a pedestal stood guard bearing a shield saying STOCKWELL BANK 1914. A plaque confirmed the year and gave the architect as Louis Sullivan, a very famous gent, Jenny Stockwell assured me. When a new modern bank came in ten years ago, her father—still president, currently chairman of the board—had shifted another of his businesses, Stockwell Insurance, into this space.

Though the building wasn't big (this was one of Sullivan's famous "jewel box" banks, Jenny said), the twenty-foot ceiling gave a sense of vastness, with a skylight and vertical side windows of stained glass letting in plenty of sun. This grand area with its mosaic floor had, however, been subdivided into a dozen or so cubicles for insurance agents. The only real office space was in back, for the executives, which is of course where Lawrence J. Stockwell, President, had his.

Jenny had accompanied me. She was something. If I ever married her, it would be for more than just her money, and not even for the part of her anatomy accurately described as a "snapper" by those who had come before me.

We had slept (under one of her nude self-portraits in a big frame) between crisp clean sheets on a waterbed, a mode of sleep I usually avoid but this was comfortable and heated, and when thanks to her I both slept in and rose early (think about it), I damn near became a convert. Her breakfast of a veggie omelette with hash browns and spice muffins made me want to burn the local Denny's down. And she had called her brother and gotten us this appointment, and left word for her father for an afternoon meet, as well.

"I think I better go with you," she'd said at breakfast. "I get along better with my brother these days, and if for some reason he gets a stick up his ass, I might be able to remove it."

"Better you than me."

I went on to the Holiday Inn to shower and shave and change for the meeting with Lawrence Stockwell. Gray blazer over a white shirt and dark tie with dark gray jeans seemed about right. Wouldn't have applied to sell insurance in that, but I was a journalist, so this should cut it.

Jenny met me in the motel lobby about eleven-forty-five and, other than the dark gypsy curls, the Pat Benatar look was M.I.A., replaced by a navy blue pantsuit with a lighter blue turtleneck.

"Well," I said, "look at you, Ms. Plastic Conservative Businesswoman."

She laughed and took my arm, walking me out. "I learned long ago, when entering the Stockwell family universe, to humor the management."

"Probably helps, if you want to stay in the Will."

"I already have a decent income, thank you, but I can't touch my trust fund principal till I'm fifty-five. If I live that long."

"It's nice to have a goal."

And maybe that explained why this free spirit had not moved away from stifling Stockwell. Always good to stay close to the money.

We were at her black Firebird in the motel parking lot. "I'm glad you didn't show up on a Harley," I said. "It's humiliating for a man, grabbing a woman from behind and holding on for dear life."

"Only if he has his clothes on," she pointed out.

She was something.

We were shown immediately into a moderately spacious cream-walled office dominated by a formidable mahogany desk with phones, blotter and the usual accessories, though no sign of work. Dark-wood file cabinets went well with the desk, as did a round polished wood table with four chairs, for client talks and business conferences.

The only thing really striking about the office were the side walls: one devoted to a dead son, the other to a missing daughter. Though this was the first I'd seen a picture of either, Lawrence Stockwell's lost children were clearly the subjects of these shrines.

Over by the table was the history of Steven Stockwell, from baby to toddler to grade schooler through junior high and high school, football, basketball, golf, prom, graduation, and at the center a studio portrait of a painfully young Marine lieutenant, with his medals (two Purple Hearts and a Bronze Star) displayed in a separate frame nearby. We'd all been so goddamn young.

The wall opposite Steven's was a memorial to Candy Stockwell. Her life from pre-school to high school was charted, though her wall was even more extreme than her brother's—a dozen color photos of various sizes, elaborately framed, charted the teenage years of a blonde who was so cute and sexy she made Barbara Eden look like Miss Hathaway. Cheerleader, musical comedy star, prom queen, with another airbrushed studio portrait center-stage, as unreal as what you see in an open casket.

Why the hell would a father put himself through the torture of surrounding himself with such raw-wound memories? Celebrating the very pursuits she so loved, and he had ultimately discouraged? The late Reed Farrell couldn't have put the guy through worse.

Taking all that in took a couple of seconds, during which Lawrence Stockwell—tall, slender, in a charcoal suit, black-and-gray striped tie—came quickly around the prop of his mahogany desk to greet his sister. He took both her hands and gave her a kiss on the cheek.

She smiled at him, tugged at an elbow of his fashionably cut loose suit coat. "Very sharp, Larry. Hugo Boss?"

He looked down at her, his smile an echo of hers. "Good eye, Sis," he said in a warm second tenor. "I only deal with the top clients these days. Gotta look the part."

He did. He was tan and trim and had the same sharp features that made his sister so striking, including the green eyes. But the black hair had gone mostly white now, trimly cut, like Johnny Carson's, with sideburns trying to keep up with the times. Though crowding fifty, he might have been sixty, making his youthful look seem a trifle desperate.

"And this is your friend Mr. Quarry," he said, turning with a smile that creased an already heavily lined face, extending a hand that I took and shook.

His firm handshake had been perfected to just the right pressure and timing over years of doing business.

"I'm pleased to get the chance to talk to you, Mr. Quarry. My sister seems to have a high opinion of you."

"We kind of hit it off," I admitted.

He gestured to the client table and we sat, with one of us on his either side. He asked if we'd like coffee or soft drinks and we declined. He leaned back in his chair and folded his arms, an ankle on a knee, so very casual. So very calculated.

"So you're a reporter with the *St. Louis Sun*?" His smile was that disguise worn by businessmen while they're assessing you.

"No," I said, raising a cautionary palm. "I don't mean to misrepresent myself. I'm strictly a freelancer. I'm still trying to place a story with the *Sun*."

Stockwell's smile continued even as his forehead frowned. "Oh? Jenny gave me to understand—"

"I'm working on a spec story for an editor at the *Sun*. I've been pitching ideas and this one generated some real interest."

I needed to make sure my cover story wouldn't crumble with a phone call.

Jenny prompted, "Jack, tell him what that idea is."

"Mr. Stockwell," I said, sitting forward just a little, "your daughter's disappearance deserves wider coverage. It garnered some attention early on, but now it's—"

"Yesterday's news," he said. His eyes were moist.

We'd just started and he was having trouble already. A haggardness became obvious. So much for his cool executive's demeanor.

"Mr. Quarry, I am glad to answer any questions you might have. So very many readers out there could relate. My daughter's disappearance…actually, I'm afraid, her *death*…is a tragedy that would touch the heart of any parent."

"I agree. But you say 'death,' and I have a feeling you mean 'murder.' Sir, I assume you're referring to the suspicions expressed by your father, in the press, about Roger Vale, your daughter's dance instructor."

He nodded slowly. That his eyes were that same clear green as Jenny's was disconcerting somehow. Clear but bloodshot.

He said, "I'm fairly confident that Dad is right about Vale's guilt. You know, Candy wrote extensively in her diary about that…that creature. He…this is difficult, Mr. Quarry, but I've had to face it. He involved her in sexual activities that were highly inappropriate. Really beyond the pale."

Jenny leaned forward and touched her brother's hand. "If that's true, Larry…that *still* wouldn't explain him killing her." She glanced at me. "Candy was seventeen when she disappeared, Jack, and seventeen is the age of consent in Missouri."

Well, if nothing else, I'd finally gathered that piece of information.

Stockwell, frowning at his sister, in frustration, not anger, said, "Maybe he wouldn't have gone to jail, but he'd have been exposed as a probable pedophile—he instructs girls as young as *twelve*, you know!"

"I just don't think," she said gently, "that you can put much stock in those diary entries. Candy was an artistic girl. You *know* that—music, dance, acting. A creative whirlwind."

I said to Jenny, "You mean, she had a crush on a gay man, and what she wrote was a fantasy of how she might…change him?"

Jenny nodded. "Why not?"

"I don't buy that at all," Stockwell said dismissively, then turned back to me and shifted the subject. "Our father hired the top investigative agencies in the country to search for Candy."

I asked, "Where have they looked?"

With a glance at his sister, he said, "We all agree that if she *had* run off, Candy would've gone somewhere to try getting into theater or some other form of show business. Those detectives have scoured New York and Los Angeles."

"There are a dozen other cities," I said, "where she might break in."

"And they've been checked, too. Mr. Quarry, I know my daughter." He paused, grimaced. "She was a lovely girl, in so many respects, but…after her mother died…she *acted out*, as they say. I may have given her too much freedom. I admit it. And…and I'm sure Jen has already told you this…I may have spoiled her somewhat. She had a very easy life here."

"Cushy as hell," Jenny said matter of factly.

"Much as I love her," he said, "I don't believe she would last out there, in the cold hard world, for more than forty-eight hours before calling me to wire her a plane ticket. Not a bus ticket, Mr. Quarry. A plane ticket. First Class."

I nodded. "Then…forgive me, sir, but…you *do* believe she's dead."

"I thought I'd made that point."

"That her body hasn't turned up doesn't give you any doubt? Or, on the other hand, hope?"

"No." He removed a handkerchief from his pocket and dried his eyes. "She's gone, Mr. Quarry. She's not out there. I can feel her absence."

He put a hand over his face for several seconds.

I asked, "Have you given any thought to the possibility that someone besides Vale may be responsible?"

The question seemed to blindside him. "Actually…no. The evidence against him is so strong that—"

"*Is* it strong?" I asked, gentle but firm. "Your family rules the roost around here. Meaning no offense, that's obvious. If there had been any solid evidence against Vale, your local District Attorney would have charged him."

"I can't argue with that. Wouldn't be the first time a shrewd killer got away with murder."

And I couldn't argue with that.

I went on: "Vale cooperated with the police. Allowed them to search his dance studio, including his living quarters. And I understand they found nothing."

Stockwell was shaking his head. "That doesn't mean anything. Vale could have somewhere he takes his victims. Some other house, some remote place."

"But *have* there been any other victims? Are any other local girls missing?"

"No," he sighed. Then he raised a lecturing forefinger. "But suppose, Mr. Quarry, suppose he's been dallying with other students, underage girls perhaps. And perhaps Candy was having an affair with him, and discovered that, became jealous, and threatened him with exposure. Statutory rape, Mr. Quarry, is no small offense. His career, his life, would be over."

"And he killed Candy to protect himself."

"Yes! Yes! And if I had my way, I'd take his skinny neck in my hands and I'd wring it like a goddamn chicken's!"

"It's an option."

Jenny got up and went to her brother and slipped an arm around him. He was trembling. "Sweetie," she said. "Sweetie. You know Candy wasn't perfect. She was headstrong and she… well, we both know she had adult desires."

He pushed her away. "Don't. Just don't."

She gave me a pained little look and returned to her chair.

"Just because *you're* that way," he said petulantly, "that doesn't mean she was."

That hit her like a slap. "You don't have to be cruel." Now *she* had tears in her eyes.

Jesus, was I the only one here who could control himself?

And Stockwell was definitely out of control, Hugo Boss threads or not. I was some reporter from Who-the-Fuck-Knew-Where, and he was threatening to strangle a dance instructor and talking trash to his sister, and I almost wished I really *was* a reporter. I'd sure have some juicy quotes.

I said, "Was your daughter dating anybody regularly at her high school?"

Stockwell nodded, distractedly, answering by rote now. "Yes. The Pettibone boy. Captain of the football team. No Rhodes scholar, but a hell of an athlete. No question he'll get major full-ride offers this year."

Jenny said, "He was an All-American high school pick as a junior. Best running back in the state."

Rah yay Stockwell High.

I said, "And he was her steady?"

"Yes."

"You mean, a not very bright lummox who thought his girl was cheating with her fruity dance instructor?"

He gave me a curdled smile. "You think *Rod Pettibone* could have murdered my daughter?"

I thought, *What wouldn't a guy named Rod Pettibone do?*

But I said, "Did the police consider him a suspect?"

"Of course not."

"Why, because he made All-American as a junior? As opposed to being a swishy dance instructor? All I'm saying is, there may be other possibilities."

He was shaking his head. "No. Not Rod. That's patently ridiculous."

Jenny leaned and said, "Larry—you *know* Candy had a lot of boyfriends. You *know* she ran around on Rod and it made him furious, but then he always came running back like a puppy."

"Maybe a rabid one this time," I said.

Stockwell seemed very tired, and a little irritated. "Mr. Quarry, if you intend with your story to whitewash Roger Vale, you are *not* going to get my cooperation. And I will advise my sister to steer you a wide path, since you've obviously misrepresented your approach to both of us."

I was shaking my head. "Sir, my approach would be journalistic. I would keep an open mind."

"Mr. Quarry…"

"All I'm saying is, the Pettibone kid is worth looking at, and any other boy she was seeing behind his back. The worst mistake you can make in an investigation is to decide at the outset who's responsible, and then try to prove it."

His chin was crinkling, quivering. "So, then, you'll go sorting through my daughter's dirty laundry?"

"If you knew the answer was in her dirty laundry, *wouldn't* you look?"

That rocked him back, and when he next spoke, he no longer seemed quite as put out with me. "Mr. Quarry, I'm sure you know this from your initial background research, but the circumstances of my daughter's disappearance are such that determining the alibis of suspects is impossible."

"Well, obviously."

Actually, I didn't know what the fuck he was talking about.

"I was out of town on a business trip that weekend," he said, forcing himself to tell it yet again. "Candy had a private lesson Saturday morning with Vale, which he admits, making him the last to report seeing her alive. She had no plans that weekend— nothing lined up with her girlfriends, nothing with Rod or any other boy that we know of. I came home Sunday afternoon and found the house empty. I wasn't alarmed. Frankly, she often went out on her own, and rarely ever left a note, so I didn't get worried till around ten o'clock that evening. When she didn't show up all night, and missed school Monday, I obviously became concerned. Hell, distraught."

"I assume the police talked to all her friends and acquaintances, to see if anyone saw her after that Saturday morning lesson."

He nodded. "And we used local paper and radio to ask if anyone had seen her. She was very well-known in the community. The only junior girl in the history of Stockwell High to be voted Queen of the Junior-Senior Prom."

And he began to cry.

To sob, both hands covering his face. A wreck of a man in Hugo Boss.

Jenny got up again and comforted him. I gave them some privacy and went over to the wall of Candy's pictures. She was a beauty, all right. Even in a photo, wholesome sex rose off her like the steamy aroma of fresh-baked bread. In her prom queen picture, she was exchanging smiles with a big broad-shouldered goofus with tiny eyes and a big stupid grin in a Big-and-Tall Store suit.

"Excuse me," I said, and pointed to the picture. "Is this Rod Pettibone?"

"It is," Stockwell said, his composure regained.

"Your daughter was petite. Almost tiny. If that clown got mad at her....Why *wasn't* he considered a suspect?"

Jenny answered that one. "Rod might be capable of violence, but he wouldn't have the brains to cover up a murder."

"Does he have parents?"

"Well, of course he has parents," Stockwell said. "His father runs the Buick dealership."

"Smart guy, Rod's old man?"

Jenny said, "Smart enough to run a Buick dealership."

"Maybe smart enough to get his kid out of a jam, too," I said, joining them at the table.

Stockwell said, "You can waste your time on the Pettibone boy if you like, Mr. Quarry. You can talk to any boy Candy dated in junior high and high school, and it's not a short list. But you'll find there's only one real suspect here—Roger Vale."

"No offense, sir, but that's an opinion based on suspicions and circumstantial evidence."

"It's much more than suspicions and circumstantial evidence," Stockwell said, "and it's more than an opinion. He *did* it."

"You state it like a fact."

Stockwell swallowed. "I shouldn't say this. Damnit, I really shouldn't." He leaned toward me, his voice hushed. "Mr. Quarry, this is *not* for publication."

So I wouldn't be able to mention it under the headline, LAWRENCE STOCKWELL THREATENS TO STRANGLE MR. ROGER. Pity.

"Agreed," I said. "And your sister's a witness."

He seemed to be tasting the words before he spoke, as if to make sure they were palatable. "My father has proof."

I frowned. "Can you share it with me?"

"I would encourage *him* to share it with you. That's the best I can do. As Jenny will tell you, our father has his own point of view on just about every subject...my daughter's death especially."

"What *is* his point of view on the subject?"

"That Vale has to be stopped." He shrugged. "All I know is that Dad's exploring options."

"Maybe *I* can be another option. For example, I can talk to Vale's other dance students and their parents."

I had no intention of doing this, of course.

I went on: "If I can uncover a pattern of sexual activity between Vale and his charges, particularly underage ones, that would bring the police back in. The Missouri state cops would pounce on the bastard. We could nail him."

He was squinting at me, trying to bring me into focus. Admittedly, I had been playing him from all sides. "Now you sound like you believe Vale is guilty, Mr. Quarry."

"Isn't it obvious?" I lied.

The door burst open as if by a gust of a wind, and a big older man, trimly gray-haired, in a well-tailored gray suit with darker gray tie, stepped in and closed the door firmly behind him, as if he owned the place.

"Dad," Stockwell said.

Oh. He did own the place.

He, too, had the sharp features of his children, though his eyes were dark—that green translucence must have been courtesy of their late mother. And his build was sturdy, no paunch, despite earned by decades of fine dining. Though he had to be at least eighty years old, his manner suggested he could still kick your ass.

Jenny was on her feet, and smiling, but I could tell she was thrown by his entrance. "Daddy. What a nice surprise. Sit down, join us. This is Mr. Quarry. I left a message—"

He came over to the table like a husband catching a cheating wife. I'd already gotten to my feet—he was the kind of guy you automatically did that for. He gave me a crocodile smile and extended a hand and his grip was a little firmer than it needed to be, possibly to show me his age wasn't a factor, or maybe he had always intimidated people like this.

"Mr. Quarry," he said, in a basso profoundo as commanding as his manner, "Clarence Stockwell. I apologize for your inconvenience."

I frowned. "My inconvenience, sir?"

"My daughter left a message at my office, wanting to bring you around this afternoon. To discuss writing a piece about my granddaughter's murder."

"Yes," I said. "I was hoping we could talk."

"Daddy," Jenny said, "please sit down."

His chin lifted and eyes that had appraised thousands of lessers over the years did the same to me. "You're with the *Sun*, I understand. I have friends over there."

"No, I'm a freelancer, sir. There's a possibility I can place a story about your granddaughter's disappearance with them."

"First of all, Mr. Quarry, it's not a disappearance. It's a murder."

"Daddy," Jenny said, "sit down, please."

He ignored her. "Second, while we appreciate your interest, the family prefers to handle this matter personally."

"Sir, I think my efforts could—"

"Mr. Quarry, this is not open for discussion. We will not be cooperating with you, and while I certainly respect the freedom of the press, I doubt without the Stockwell family's cooperation that you can get very far."

"Sir, with the right media coverage, we can expose Roger Vale for the monster he is."

He regarded me with a skeptical smile. "So you're convinced that fiend murdered my granddaughter?"

"I am, after talking to your son. After all, he says you have *proof*...."

The old man shot his son a blast-furnace glare, and the tall insurance exec seemed to shrink.

"I didn't say anything, Dad," Lawrence Stockwell said. He might have been ten.

Clarence Stockwell appeared to be finished with me. He swung to his daughter and said, "Jennifer, please remove your young friend from this office. I understand you mean well, dear, but I have this situation in hand."

"Daddy..."

"Go. Now."

We went.

Outside, in the chilly fall air, she huddled next to me, her arm through mine. "He's a charmer, my father."

"Force of nature, I'd say."

"Are you discouraged?"

"No, I still plan to work on the story. You aren't cutting me off, are you?"

She managed a little smile. "Cutting you off from what?"

"Nothing, I hope. Why don't you take me somewhere nice for lunch? I'll even let you pay. You can get back at your father that way."

She took me to the Golden Spike for cheeseburgers and fries, but she did pay. I'll give her that.

Anyway, I had a problem, and it wasn't that Clarence Stockwell wasn't cooperating with me. He'd cooperated just fine. That he had hired the contract was damn near a lock. The question was, was his son in on it? In which case, Lawrence Stockwell would have to go, as well.

I felt kind of bad about it, for two reasons. First, Lawrence seemed like a decent guy and his death would be tough on Jenny. And second, how could I get away with going back to Vale for a higher fee, at this point?

Might have to kill two Stockwells for the price of one.

EIGHT

About two o'clock, Jenny dropped me off in the Holiday Inn parking lot. She wondered if I wanted to go out somewhere tonight, and I said love to, but I had some business things that needed attending—we'd get together tomorrow, if she was free.

I couldn't break it to her that I already had a date with a teen-age girl.

Lingering in the lot, I watched her drive off in that Batmobile of a Firebird, thinking what an incredible woman she was, when I noticed a familiar vehicle pull in across the way, at the Rest Haven Court.

Funny, I thought, *you wouldn't think there were that many shit-brown Bonnevilles around....*

And there weren't, because as I watched, that Bonneville slowed near Cabin 12, hesitated at the sight of the vacant space outside it, then pulled into it.

Climbing out of the Pontiac was an unmistakable chunky redheaded guy in a gray quilted ski jacket and jeans—not that many of those around, either.

Looking around with confusion and caution, he walked to the cabin door. He knocked. He pounded. Then stood there with hands on hips, looking exasperated, glancing side to side and then behind him, finally climbing back into the Bonneville and pulling out of the Rest Haven lot.

If he had turned left and headed for Highway 218, I'd have jumped in the Pinto and taken off after him. Right then and there.

But he didn't.

He was heading into town, presumably to find his partner. After all, other than maybe a restaurant or two—and we were well past the lunch hour—Farrell could only be one place, really.

Staking out Roger Vale's dance studio.

Why had Mateski returned?

Obviously he had tried to check in with his active half by phone, maybe even at a designated time, and Farrell (being dead) didn't answer. Maybe Mateski had then checked in with their middleman and been told to go back to Stockwell and see what the fuck was up. More likely Mateski hadn't taken that step yet, not wanting to send up a red flag to a middleman who might accuse the team of screwing up.

And now the antiques dealer had found no sign of his partner at the motel, which could mean only one of two things: Farrell was carrying out the hit, right this minute…or something had gone very wrong.

The former might seem improbable to Mateski, since this was daylight, and a nighttime scaling of the dance instructor's fortress made more sense. Of course, this was a torture kill, and who knew how long Farrell might take with that task. Or *where* he might carry out his gruesome mission….

Which meant Mateski might have a secondary location to check out, some safe house (so to speak) where Farrell was even now snipping off dance-instructor toes or testicles or what-have-you. Maybe Farrell hadn't checked in by phone with Mateski because he was having so much darn fun, he lost track of time.

Bottom line was: Farrell had not fucking checked in with Mateski, or been available for a designated call, which put the kill unexpectedly behind schedule. And the team had presumably agreed that Mateski would return in such an event, to provide whatever back-up might be needed.

A thousand questions would be racing through Mateski's mind—*what could have gone wrong? If Farrell was still staking out the target, why the hell was he? Had Mateski overlooked something? Had the target gotten the better of Farrell somehow, and was the wrong man getting a gonad-ectomy?*

I had a thousand questions racing through my mind, too. Some of them I've already shared, but the major one was whether to climb in the Pinto and follow Mateski, right now.

After perhaps half a minute of mulling that there in the chilly parking lot, I decided not to. I knew very damn well that Mateski would not find Farrell staking out Vale, or in a torturer's hideaway, either. The only place Ronald Mateski might find Reed Farrell was in the morgue at the county hospital, where he was not likely to look.

Which meant once Mateski had figured out that Farrell was nowhere he should be—not the motel or the dance studio or the safe house (if there even was one)—he would head home. Back to Highway 218. Past the Holiday Inn.

Right by me.

I went up to my room and got out of the blazer but left on the same jeans. Changed from the white shirt and tie into a sweatshirt. I put the hunting knife on my belt and climbed into the fleece-lined jacket, then tucked the noise suppressor in my left pocket and the nine mil in the right. Much as I dislike knives, the switchblade might come in handy, so I stuck that in my right jeans pocket.

In the parking lot, I backed the Pinto around to where I had the closest space to the exit, with the nose facing out. And I sat and I watched. Fifteen minutes passed and they couldn't have seemed longer at an art movie with no nude scenes.

Finally, the brown Bonneville rolled into my line of vision and into the Rest Haven lot, as well. He pulled up in front of the manager's cabin, and I frowned. That was interesting…and risky, if he was going to do what I thought he might.

And he did: he headed up the sidewalk to the manager's cabin.

This seemed potentially a bad fucking move. Mateski had checked in—and Farrell had checked out—almost certainly under the same name. If whoever was at the desk in there recognized Mateski, a lot of dangerous questions might get asked, and not just by the management of the Rest Haven Court.

Two guests sharing one room and one name, with one of those guests dying in his sleep (maybe), got even the laziest small-town cop thinking.

But then I noticed that the redhead was pausing to bend and look through the door glass to see who was at the desk.

Okay, I thought, *you're making sure it's not the same clerk who checked you in. If it isn't, if it's someone you never dealt with here at the Rest Haven, you're good to go…*

He went. Into the manager's cabin, that is.

I got out of the car, and picked my way through traffic until I was across the street. I trotted down and up the ditch and onto the Rest Haven's overgrown dead lawn. In front of God and everybody, I went to the side window and carefully peeked in, exposing as little of myself to view from within as possible.

Mateski, showing no sign of anything being wrong, was talking to a plain-looking dishwater blonde with glasses, skinny in a University of Missouri sweatshirt and jeans. It was just that classy a joint. Not wanting to be seen by Mateski, I was at a slant that gave me the clerk from the front, angled right, with the antiques dealer's back largely to me.

Lip-reading gave me her side of the conversation:

I'm terribly sorry to have to give you this bad news, sir, but your friend in number twelve passed away in his sleep Sunday night.

Now Mateski, after a pause to process that, spoke. Too muffled for me to pick anything out, and not enough of the side of
his face for me to read his lips.

Then (she was a chatty thing, and this isn't exact): *I wasn't
on duty, but I understand it was a heart attack. I'm afraid that's
all I know. Must be just terrible to show up for a meeting with
somebody, and to get news like this. I'm so sorry. Would you
like me to dial the police, so you can talk to them about it?*

Apparently he didn't, because he just nodded thanks, and
went back out the door. By the time he'd exited, I'd tucked
myself behind the cabin, and from there I saw his Bonneville
roll out of the Rest Haven lot, taking a left.

Toward Highway 218.

Again, I ran down into and up out of the ditch, then across
the street, dancing around traffic, got into the Pinto, and took
off after him.

By the time I picked him up, two cars were already between
us, so that was good. I was concerned that after I'd followed
him out of town Sunday night, he might have noticed the Pinto.
I probably should have picked something less conspicuous—
shitty clunker cars, in their way, can be as noticeable as luxury
rides and sportier vehicles.

As expected, he turned north on 218. Presumably he was
heading home, to Woodstock. He was not speeding, more like
slowpoking it, and I had to work to keep at least one car between
us. He was probably distracted, trying to figure out what the
fuck was going on. I got more than my share of dirty looks and
an occasional middle finger from drivers stuck behind me till
they could pass and do me the favor of getting between me
and the Bonneville.

The afternoon was overcast, more like dusk than mid-
afternoon, and the sky was grumbling, as if it were as annoyed

as I was, having to follow this cocksucker again. Right now my chief worry was not being made—I even had close to a full tank of gas.

But if he was going all the way back to Woodstock, I would have to fill up at some point. Doing so at the same time, and same place, as Mateski was risky as hell. And stopping at some station while letting him go on ahead without me was riskier still.

After all, I couldn't be certain he was heading back to Woodstock. All I knew for sure was that he was driving north on 218. If I stopped for fuel, I could lose him. Like if he took a detour to meet with his middleman.

Also, he might stop and use a pay phone, either at a gas station or some booth somewhere, to call that middleman and tell him that the hit had gone sour. I didn't want that redheaded bastard to make a phone call like that. The complications that might cause me meant I would probably have to scrap the job.

I did not turn on the car radio this time. I was in no mood for oldies, and the New Wave that was the only current music I could tolerate was too fucking frantic. I needed to stay focused. My brain was alive with possibilities, and I don't mean positive ones.

What did Mateski showing up mean?

Not in the literal sense of why exactly was he here and the mechanics of that, no. Whatever had brought him back to Stockwell, he *had* come back to fucking Stockwell. This much I knew. And Farrell was dead—that much *he* knew. Before long, he would tell the middleman, and the middleman would report to Clarence Stockwell or whoever-the-fuck had taken out the torture contract.

Should I be doing what Mateski was—heading home?

I could pack my clothes and my toiletries and my weapons

and just check out of the Holiday Inn, possibly but not necessarily giving Vale a courtesy call saying I had to bail. Good luck, Mr. Roger. Happy beauty pageants.

Might even have time to stop and say goodbye to Jenny. I had a feeling she could throw a guy a hell of a goodbye.

But, goddamnit, I had invested time and money in this job, including removing that prick Farrell. I don't kill people for my amusement or to stay in practice—it's got to pay off, or what's the fucking point?

Since I'd begun plumbing the Broker's list for potential clients among targets, I never had to pull the plug. Not once. I'd always managed to come through for my client, no matter how dicey things got. There's such a thing as professional pride.

We crossed into Iowa, and around four-thirty, Mateski did something I never expected, although really I should have. Even a boring asshole can surprise you now and then.

Outside Iowa City, he pulled into a small parking lot by a low-slung building, a modern prefab number, with HAWKEYE ANTIQUES painted on its slanting roof in bright red letters. Only one other car was in the parking lot, a new-looking Chevy pickup truck with *Hawkeye Antiques* painted on the door.

Mateski was already inside when I pulled in. It was almost dark, dusk and the overcast sky collaborating on an early evening. A single gas lamp on a pole did a shitty job of lighting the gravel lot, but then the sign on the door said HOURS — 10 A.M. TO 5 P.M., so Hawkeye Antiques didn't have a nighttime business.

I pulled in next to the Bonneville.

When I went in, an overhead bell ringing, I couldn't see Mateski. It was a typical antiques mall with stalls arranged in narrow aisles going horizontally. At my left, behind a long checkout counter with a glass case of pricier collectibles, was a youngish guy who looked half hippie, half farmer (long hair,

John Deere cap). He wore a gray Hawkeye Antiques t-shirt and frayed jeans. Barely looking at me, he said, "Closing soon, still time to look."

I nodded my thanks, and began down the first aisle, turning right. Coming back around the second aisle, I spotted Mateski, halfway down, looking over the top of his amber-tinted glasses to check out an ugly painting.

That was just like this son of a bitch. He knows his hit has gone south, he knows his partner is dead, he *has* to know he should tell his middleman or, if they worked direct with the client, warn whoever hired him.

But he was also an antiques dealer, and all antiques dealers are antiques junkies, and here he was with a great big Bonneville with a great big empty trunk and a passenger-less back seat, so what's the harm, stopping to pick out a few treasures from the trash?

He apparently decided that this painting came too close to actually resembling something, so he put it back on its nail, and pressed on. I lagged behind. He didn't seem to have noticed me. This time, though, I didn't bother browsing. I would have, if any other patrons were in the shop. But we had the place to ourselves, Mateski and I, just two pros in the killing business and one hippie-farmer kid.

Halfway down the next aisle, Mateski found a small table that looked like it might fall apart under a teacup, and he held it up like a gem he was checking for flaws. But this primitive piece of shit apparently had no flaws whatsoever, because he clutched it to him like a beautiful woman, and all but ran to the end of the aisle and turned left. I could hear him telling the hippie-farmer to hold it for him.

When he resumed his shopping, I had tucked myself within a booth where some old books were on sale, with high, wide bookcases I could duck behind. I spotted a few Louis L'Amours, but I wasn't buying today.

I peeked out from the stall and he was gone, but then I heard him in the next aisle over, fiddling with shit.

Was I being suckered by this prick?

Had he seen me following him? Had he led me here, to this almost deserted spot, to kill my idiot ass? The hippie-farmer would be collateral damage, but that would be acceptable to Mateski, considering the circumstances. Plus, he'd get his primitive crap free.

Was I the hunter, or the small-q quarry here?

In the next aisle he found a ghastly barn-wood painting of a farmhouse, and this, too, he carried to the front counter like an emerald from the tomb of King Tut. This process continued in each remaining aisle—two more paintings, one of a church (I think), another of a rooster (maybe), a rag doll suitable for voodoo pins, and an unpainted carved bird.

In the rear aisle, a door to a unisex bathroom stood open. We were both in that aisle—he was studying some ungainly looking wooden spoons—and I wondered if I could just grab him, chuck him into that john and kill *his* idiot ass.

Well, obviously I could. But what about that clerk? Like I said, collateral damage was not my deal—too sloppy. And anyway, what did that kid do to deserve to die, besides wear that John Deere cap?

So I stood in the aisle on the other side of which was the checkout counter. I listened while the clerk rang Mateski up—$292.67 for items worthy of a garbage dump—and waited for the sound of the bell over the door to announce Mateski's exit.

The farmer-hippie kid did not glance at me—he was too busy checking out the afternoon's proceeds in the till—as I stood at the door glass, watching Mateski, who was uncomfortably nearby, in the closest parking place. He stuck the furniture in the back seat—it took some juggling—then, carrying them by their wire hangers, carted the paintings behind the Bonneville, and opened the trunk.

As I went out, the clerk, without even a glance at me, said, "Thanks for looking, come again," and I moved quickly around behind the Bonneville, in back of Mateski, the car's trunk lid up. He sensed the movement but not quickly enough. I already had the switchblade in my right hand and I clicked it, blade jumping as I shoved him forward with my left, and when I cut his throat, the arterial blood sprayed forward, into the trunk, on the underside of the lid and into the trunk itself and on top of the small stack of paintings, adding more color to the faded primitive farmhouse on top.

I got almost none of it on me, just a little on my right hand.

Big though he was, stuffing him in that trunk was no problem, and the blood spray quickly stopped, because his heart wasn't pumping anymore, so there was no risk of me getting spattered, though it was still messy enough that I had to be careful. My hand I wiped off on his trousers.

His car keys were in his jacket pocket. I removed them, shut the trunk, unlocked the Bonneville's driver-side door, slid behind the wheel, and drove slowly out of the lot. The clerk was just a few yards from all this, but inside, counting cash, his back to the window, and there'd been precious little noise. Even if he'd glanced out, all he'd have seen was the raised trunk lid of a customer storing away precious purchases.

I drove only a quarter mile or so before pulling into a dirt access lane to a farmer's field. Corn looked high and ready for harvest. Good yield this year. I hadn't worn surgical gloves, so I used my untucked sweatshirt to rub off the steering wheel and where I'd touched the trunk.

This far from Stockwell, hell this far from Missouri, the body with a slit throat in the trunk of a Bonneville would be a source of attention for local and state cops, but with no likelihood of coming back on me.

Yet whoever had hired Mateski and Farrell, whether directly or through a middleman, was still out there wanting my client dead. How long I had to keep that from happening, I had no idea. A ticking clock is bad enough. What if you don't know what the fuck it's counting down?

At least Mateski himself was out of my life now, not to mention his.

So I was pleased with how this went, even if I did still find killing with a knife nothing I wanted to make a habit out of.

These were my thoughts as I walked back briskly to the antiques shop. The clerk was still in the window, his back to me, counting cash. I got in the Pinto and made tracks.

I had a date at six o'clock.

Mustang Sally was taking me to a parent–teacher meeting.

NINE

The west side of Stockwell, sprawling with recent high-end housing developments, was home to the Horace J. Stockwell Senior High School. Built in 1976, it replaced the previous "new" Horace J. Stockwell Senior High built in 1948, now used for the Isaac R. Stockwell Junior High. What became of the previous Horace J. Stockwell Senior High never came up. Maybe there'd been several. Who could get enough of Horace J. Stockwell Senior Highs?

"But nobody calls it that," Sally told me, at the wheel of her baby-blue Mustang. The interior was pink. "Just Stockwell High. You know?"

She had picked me up at six-thirty at the Holiday Inn, and I was getting to like having hot-looking females drive me around.

"Who was Horace J.?" I asked her.

We were pulling into the big parking lot of the massive tan-brick complex, two wide modern-looking stories bookended by an auditorium and a field house—an impressive facility. Either local taxes were high or the Stockwell family was a friend to education.

"I think he invented the buggy whip or something," Sally said. "Or maybe that was Isaac. Before my time, you know?"

She was pulling into a space near the front. We were one of only a score or so of cars. Parent–teacher night was apparently not a big draw.

"I'm not a local," she reminded me, "you know?"

She was a lovely girl, even if she did attach "you know" to

everything she said. You know? But what red-blooded high-school boy wouldn't overlook an annoying vocal habit for all that frizzy tawny hair, those big blue eyes, that pug nose and those plump cherry-lipsticked lips, puckering naturally, an effect heightened by a slight overbite.

Tonight Sally Meadows was dressed conservatively, at least compared to the girls-just-wanna-have-fun wardrobe from Vale's digs the other day—a navy-red-and-white plaid dress with a thrift store cowboy belt under a brown tweed blazer with leather elbow patches and collar, and purposely clunky-looking navy sneakers with white laces. The plaid dress, a tad longer than mini-length, vaguely said Catholic school girl uniform, which as fashion statements went seemed to me a pretty damn good one.

I, by the way, was back in journalist mode, white shirt, dark tie, and gray jeans, the fleece-lined jacket over that. No guns in the pockets tonight. Or knives either.

"Listen, Jack," she said. We'd already agreed I would call her Sally and she would call me Jack. "I've never been to one of these stupid nights, you know? So I'm gonna be moving quick past some of these classrooms."

"Okay. Who do you think I should be talking to?"

"Strictly the artsy-fartsy crowd—Mr. Dennis, drama, Miss Hurlbutt, cheerleading, actually she's a gym teacher, you know? Mr. Brady, school newspaper, Mr. Jacobs, swing choir."

"Seems like Candy was involved in just about all the arts at Stockwell High."

"Not *just* about all, *all*, you know? She even took art class, drawing and shit, but that teacher's not worth talking to—just the ones involved with pageant prep."

"Pageant prep—getting girls ready to participate in Miss Teenage Missouri and the like?"

She bobbed her frizzy head. "Right. And for Candy to take all that creative junk, she had to get special dispensation, you know?"

"What?"

"There's a limit at HSSH on how many arts any student can get involved in."

HSSH appeared to be another name for Stockwell High.

She was saying, "Because her family pours so much into the school and stuff, not just arts but athletics…the Yellow Jackets *rule* in this part of the state…the administrators made an exception for Candy. She could take all the arts classes and activities she wanted."

"The Yellow Jackets—that's the name of the football team?"

"And basketball and baseball, any HSSH teams."

A few parents were heading into the school with unhappy teenagers in tow, as the girl and I sat in her car, talking.

"Sally, did Candy getting paid all this special attention make her…unpopular around school?"

She put a finger to a cheek—pink fingernail polish. "Well, I was probably the only *close* friend Candy had around school, you know? I was really into dance like her, and we kind of clicked right from jump street, over at Roger's studio. I call him Roger because we're friends. But I call him 'Mr. Vale' in front of the other girls."

"Probably wise. So, then, she was *unpopular* with her classmates?"

She frowned in thought. "No. It's hard to explain. She was *envied*, that's for sure. And I think she was probably hated. But not *unpopular*, you know?"

"I don't know, Sally. Explain it to me."

"Well…let me ask you this. Do you think I'm good-lookin'? Kinda cute, wouldja say?"

I would have set fire to the Sistine Chapel, for a half an hour with her.

I said, "You're a very attractive girl, Sally."

"Thank you. I think I probably am, by most yardsticks. But if Candy was here—if I was standing over there and she was standing next to me, right now? You wouldn't even notice me. It would be like I wasn't even *there*, you know?"

"Did *you* like her?"

She swallowed, nodded bravely. "I loved her. She was misunderstood. Because I came in from out of town, a new kid and all? And didn't have any…you know, baggage from grade school and junior high, we hit off. Like I say, we were *really* into dance classes, but I don't have any ambitions for Miss Teenage Missouri or anything, so I wasn't any competition to Candy."

"Why aren't you part of the pageant scene? You'd be a natural."

"I'm just not into it—kind of phony baloney, I think. But my opinion isn't important. You're trying to understand *Candy*, right?"

"Right."

"Well, a girl like Candy—so beautiful, with all those designer clothes, so totally talented, a cheerleader and prom queen and everything—*that's* somebody other girls wanna get next to."

"Even if nobody notices them standing beside her?"

"You still want to bask in it. Add to that how rich she was, who her family was, and you bet other girls wanted to be around her. Be seen as part of her clique. Only she really didn't *have* a clique, you know, other than the two of us hanging out."

"Was she nice to other girls? I hear she was a spoiled brat at home—maybe she was a brat at school, too."

"I guess she kind of was. She could seem stuck-up. She had to have her way, you know? She knew how good she was, how pretty, how smart, how talented. But she wasn't mean. Not a bitch or anything."

"What about guys?"

She smiled and rolled the big blue eyes. "*All* the guys loved her. All the guys *wanted* her."

"And I understand a lot of them got her."

That got a nod and a smirk out of her. "Candy was no tease. I mean…she put out. She *liked* doing it. She bragged about how good she was at, you know…head? She didn't think there was anything wrong with having a good time."

"And that didn't cause her any trouble?"

Her perfectly plucked eyebrows rose. "She broke a lot of hearts. She'd be with a guy for a month, then dump him. And after giving him…everything. Drove 'em bananas. And she would have little flings on the side. If she had an argument with her steady, Rod, he's captain of the football team and a *real* hunk, she would use that as an excuse to run around on him. She could be a total bimbette sometimes."

"How did Rod take that?"

"How do you think?"

"I saw a picture of him. He looks like a big guy, a real bruiser. Did he ever hit her? Hurt her?"

Frowning, she shook her head. "Oh, no, he's a real pussycat when he's not playing sports. He would yell at her and even cry—he's very *romantic*, you know?"

"You know Rod well, do you?"

"Oh, we've been dating. I suppose *I'm* his steady now."

That had me blinking.

She picked up, "I can arrange so you can talk to him. He's very nice. He's no rocket surgeon, but he's got a good heart. Might be here tonight. Grades are always an issue with Rod."

"Color me shocked."

"Do I sense disapproval, Jack? I know I'm a kind of substitute Candy for him. I'm no fool. I know he's drawn to me because I was her best friend." She swallowed and winced. "I hate talking about her like she's gone."

"She is gone."

"I mean…talking about her in the third person. Like she's… dead."

"I think she probably is."

She glanced off to her right, where the lights of Stockwell's housing developments were the only stars twinkling tonight, thanks to the grumbling overcast sky. "Candy could be out there somewhere, couldn't she…? She *could* be?"

"You're right," I said. She seemed on the edge of tears. "We don't know for sure.…Hey, let's go in."

We walked up the big wide sidewalk. She looped her arm in mine. She only came up to my shoulder. "Listen, if anybody asks, you're my Uncle Jack. My aunt's brother from out of town."

"You live with your aunt?"

"My mother's dead," she said with a nod. "Father, too. And you're doing a story on Candy's disappearance for…what paper is it?"

"The *St. Louis Sun*. You seem to have this all figured out, Sally."

"Actually, Roger did. He ran me through it. He's a wonderful teacher."

"Not everybody thinks so," I reminded her, opening one of the heavy steel doors.

"Oh, everybody knows he's a wonderful teacher," she said, stepping inside. "It's just that some people think he's also a sex killer, you know?"

The school was as modern within as without, and the kind of money spent here was perhaps best represented by the huge fancy mosaic cartoon bumblebee you saw upon entering, engulfing the facing wall. The Yellow Jackets ruled in Stockwell.

Sally escorted me around the school. Either on her own or at Roger Vale's prompting, she had very efficiently made appointments with each of Candy's teachers deemed the appropriate ones for me to interview. Like the real parent–teacher meetings this evening, I'd be limited to fifteen minutes each.

I was fine with that. I was breaking a rule, or at least ignoring an important strategy, being this visible in a town where I was working. But spending a few minutes with people, in my journalist pose, shouldn't make too great an impression. I hoped.

My looks were inoffensively pleasant enough to allow me to get laid occasionally, then run into a woman a year later and maybe not get recognized. I could be sitting next to you on the plane as you read this, or in the next deck chair by a hotel pool, and we'd smile and nod and exchange words about the weather, and I'd be gone from your memory by tomorrow. Sooner.

Still, I was here to ask questions about a missing girl, and not just *any* missing girl, but Candy Stockwell, prom queen/beauty pageant contender/most popular girl/notorious slut/envied/ talented/hated/spoiled/rich (but not, Sally insisted, a bitch). Maybe alive, probably dead.

So I just might be remembered.

Candy may have been as good an actress as her drama teacher would soon insist, but I didn't think she could have been any better than Sally. At every stop, little Miss Meadows introduced me as her uncle who was doing an article on Candy's disappearance. She asked to be forgiven for scheduling the appointment on the false pretense of a parent–teacher talk, but her uncle would only be around for a few days and she would really, really appreciate it if they could help him out, you know?

Then she would smile sweetly and prance out in all her schoolgirlish pleated glory. So effective was this exit that it became my method of determining my interviewee's sexual preference and predilection for fooling around with a student, gauged by whether a teacher watched her entire departure, and if so, what expression that teacher wore.

Not exactly fair, but unlike teachers, assassins can't lose their certification.

Mr. Dennis liked to conduct his parent–teacher talks on the stage of the impressive Clyde S. Stockwell Auditorium. He had set up three director's chairs next to a little table with a water pitcher and some paper cups. He was in his late fifties or early sixties, and I pegged him as gay when he didn't glance at Sally's exit, which had seemed particularly impressive on stage.

"Thank you for putting up with this imposition," I said, giving him a businesslike smile.

Our voices echoed a little in the auditorium.

"Not at all," he said. "I am pleased to see some movement on this matter. We were all just starting to give up hope."

He had an oblong, well-lined face with regular features, his head large for his slender frame. His eyes were gray and languid behind dark-frame glasses and his steel-gray hair was immaculately cut and combed. He wore a black sweater over a gray shirt with a red bow tie; his darker gray slacks had a nice crease, and he was in black slippers.

Throughout our brief interview, he clasped his hands in front of his chest, fingers entwined, and made his points emphatically, even when emphasis wasn't required, as if he were giving me pointers on my performance.

"Will you be taking notes, Mr. Quarry?"

"No, I'll make my notes after we talk. Anyway, I don't intend to quote you by name."

"Ah. Merely as a source. I see. That's actually a relief."

"I thought it might be. I'll be asking some questions that require opinions, and hope you will express frankly any suspicions or theories you might have. Without risk of putting yourself in a compromising position."

"All right. I like the sound of that. Have you the Stockwell family's by-their-leave to pursue this line of inquiry?"

"Jenny Stockwell is helping me. She arranged an interview with her brother Lawrence earlier today. Her father has declined to speak to me."

He nodded. "Yes. That is no surprise. By all accounts, the elder Stockwell is devastated, and who could blame him?"

"Was Candy the talented girl everyone says she was?"

"Very gifted. Her sophomore year she was excellent in *Skin of Our Teeth*. The last two years we've done musicals in conjunction with swing choir, and she nabbed leads in both—*Godspell* and *Pippin*."

"You're involved in helping prepare some of the girls for beauty pageant competition?"

"Yes. It's a fairly barbaric, painfully out-of-date tradition, but I'm afraid it's terribly popular in Stockwell, and when in Rome…."

"So you know Roger Vale, then?"

"I know Roger. He's very gifted."

"You've worked with him?"

"Yes, a consummate professional. And I will save you the trouble of asking your next question—no, I do *not* believe he had anything to do with Candace's disappearance. As much as I appreciate how the Stockwell family supports the arts in this community, I believe they…particularly Clarence…are bogged down in old attitudes. They have a prejudice toward Roger that fogs their judgment."

"You mean, because he's gay."

He raised his chin and looked down his nose at me. "I suppose he *might* be gay, but I can tell you flatly, in dealing with him, many times, I have to say it never came up."

Sometimes a straight line is just too easy.

"But," I said, "you assume that *they* assume he's gay."

"That's fair. That *is* fair. You might find this difficult to believe, but I deal with the same prejudice. Just because I am involved in the theater arts. Actually, I am a happily and long-married man. Ethel is head librarian at the Stockwell Library."

"Congratulations. Do you think it's possible that Candy is a runaway?"

Hands still clasped, he pondered. "I don't believe so. We were fairly close, Candace and I. I was helping her explore various college options, seeking programs that might serve *all* of her gifts—dance, vocal music and of course drama. She never gave the slightest indication that she might be considering running off to try for Broadway or film. She was smarter than that. She was many things, our Candace, but stupid was not one of them."

"If she was murdered, who might have done it?"

The languid eyes flared suddenly. "*Must* it have been someone local? Couldn't she have been spirited off by some maniac who saw the lovely girl and simply had to have her?"

"Just some crazy killer drifting around America, looking for high school girls to kidnap and kill."

"And *more*, Mr. Quarry. And more. What debauchery that poor child may have suffered before facing a tragic death boggles. The heights of the human soul have no ceiling, and the lows of its depravity no floor."

"Who said that, Shakespeare?"

"No, Mr. Quarry," he said, and smiled like a pixie. "I did. Just now."

Miss Hurlbutt, the cheerleading coach, sat with me in the gymnasium on the first row of the bleachers. She was in a yellow Yellow Jacket sweatshirt and black sweatpants, as if she'd just come from practice. The ponytailed bottle blonde was apple-cheeked and about forty, with her weight just starting to be a problem. But with that dimpled smile, who gave a shit?

She shook her head, watching Sally's exit. "*There's* a waste."

"Pardon?"

"Ever see that kid dance, that Sally? She's a natural. But I have had *zero* luck recruiting her for cheer. I hate seeing potential go unrealized. So what can I do you for?"

I gave her the standard spiel, and again invoked Jenny Stockwell as a reference.

"Listen," she said, "Candy was a hard worker. This talk about her being a stuck-up little bitch, buncha bull. She interacted well with the other girls. Team player."

"I don't suppose there's any room for a diva in cheerleading."

"You got that right. And I admired Candy for that, because she was a star, if this school ever had one. Best actress HSSH ever saw, fantastic soloist in swing choir, and she stole every darn recital out at Vale Dance Studio."

"You know Roger Vale?"

She nodded. "Mr. Roger has lent a hand helping my girls, the ones who're prepping for pageants. Oh, I know it's a bunch of sexist baloney, but it's a way a girl can get some confidence ...*and* a nice scholarship."

"Candy Stockwell didn't need a nice scholarship."

"That's for dang sure. But she needed *something*, or else she wouldn't have participated, would she?"

"What do you mean, Miss Hurlbutt?"

"Make it Judy, please. And I'll take the liberty of calling you, Jack...Jack. Any young beauty who tries as hard, works as hard as Candy, has self-esteem issues."

"Why the hell *would* she, Judy?"

"You got me by the short-and-you-know-whats. Look at some of these pretty girls who won't eat, or when they do, they puke, and wind up looking like concentration camp victims. Some of the prettiest, most talented girls have the lowest self-esteem, Jack. I think that's probably why Candy...well, got around."

"People I've talked to have called her a slut."

"That's of course cruel, and maybe an exaggeration."

Maybe.

I said, "What's it like, working with Roger Vale?"

"He's a dream. Strictly professional, and Mr. Roger has more talent in his little pinkie than me or anybody else on the HSSH staff."

"The Stockwells—Clarence and his son Lawrence, anyway— don't share your high opinion of Vale. They think he murdered Candy."

Her cheerful persona vanished. She seemed genuinely sorrowful, shaking her head as she said, "It's a shame, a damn shame. Town is so lucky to have that family. But the old man, old Clarence, he's grasping at straws, trying to make sense out of a tragedy."

"You don't think Candy might be a runaway?"

"No. She was on a path to college. We talked about that, many times. No. I'm afraid something terrible did happen to her."

"But not at the hands of Roger Vale?"

"That gentle soul? No. I would imagine it's his sexual orientation that sends them down that dark path. He doesn't flaunt it, you know. Oh, yes, he can be a little…effeminate."

"No worse than Paul Lynde."

That made her chuckle and shrug in a you-got-me-there fashion. "I mean, Roger keeps to himself. If he's had any affairs here in town, he's been awful discreet. He might go out of town for his social life, for all I know. But it's a terrible, judgmental thing he's suffering."

"You mean, he'd have been better off marrying a librarian."

She laughed out loud at that one. "You have a dry sense of humor, Jack. How long are you in town?"

"Not long enough," I said with a smile, and we passed like ships in the night, or anyway the gym.

Mr. Brady—the fortyish Lincoln-esque history teacher who was the advisor on the school newspaper—echoed the comments of Mr. Dennis and Miss Hurlbutt, as we sat in student chairs in his classroom.

But he added, "Candy was a very good writer. Extremely creative. You know, her aunt is talented, too—a painter, a musician, and she's in my writing group."

"You're a member?"

"No, I'm sort of the…ringleader, or maybe ring*master*. But this notion of Mr. Vale being Candy's murderer…and course, where is the *body*?…is fueled by this diary that the elder Stockwell so cruelly allowed to be excerpted in the local press. Salacious material that had to be censored to some degree, but had Mr. Vale ever been brought to trial locally, think how poisoned the jury pool would be."

"I think those diary entries do play a big role."

"Without a doubt. And they were almost certainly fantasies of hers put to paper, and as I say, she was a very gifted young writer. The assumption of Mr. Vale's guilt, of a crime that hasn't been demonstrated to have *occurred*, is an outrageous miscarriage of justice."

"Well, Vale hasn't been arrested. And he doesn't even seem to have been convicted in the court of public opinion. Poisoned jury pool maybe, Mr. Brady, but a lot of parents who have girls taking dance lessons at his studio seem to have his back."

"I don't know if that's a good indicator," he said. "Whether they stick a knife in that back may well depend on which and how many of our Stockwell girls place well in the coming beauty pageants. This town is so obsessed by that antique display that they would have a kind word for Caligula, if he was an effective dance coach."

The swing choir director, his heterosexuality clear after that lingering look at Sally's skirt-swishing exit, continued with praise

for Candy's talent, and backed up the general high opinion of
Roger Vale.

Mr. Jacobs was a small pale dark-haired man in a dark suit
and dark tie, sitting sideways at his desk with me seated directly
across from him. Around us was auditorium-style seating, indicating a choir of healthy size.

"Roger Vale has been so helpful to me," Mr. Jacobs said, "I
wouldn't know where to start. Swing choir is relatively new at
Stockwell High, Mr. Quarry, and I don't know how much you
know about it...?"

"I know nothing about it."

"Well, it brings in elements of dance, and my college training
did *not* include anything like that. Much more traditional, I'm
afraid, and Mr. Vale has been a lifesaver. Very professional with
the students—boys and girls, and I assure you his...lifestyle
choice...did not manifest itself in the way he coached our
young men. Who, as you might imagine, can be fairly shy about
learning dance steps."

"You don't put any stock in the accusations made against
Vale, by Clarence Stockwell, as Candy's possible murderer?"

"I don't. They *can't* have it both ways—is 'Mr. Roger' some
pervert because he's gay? Or is he some mad sex fiend deflow-
ering young girls? May I be frank, Mr. Quarry? Speak to you as
one man to another. Frankly?"

"Please."

"And you *assure* me I won't be quoted?"

"Yes."

He sighed, shook his head. "Candy was a stone fox. I was alone
with her any number of times. Many times. I could have...well, I
could have. I didn't, I have a lovely young wife I'm madly in love
with, but...my God, I would think about her at night, Candy...
who wouldn't want..."

"A piece of Candy?" You knew I'd get there.

He smiled humorlessly. "I've said too much. But she was the kind of beauty who could make a man crazy. Men *kill* over women who look like that. Who have that, that *well* of…passion."

Was he *sure* that he…hadn't?

"Anyway, I'm just saying that she gave a lot away to a host of stupid boys who didn't deserve it. Somebody…some kid maybe, filled with hormonal lust and teenage angst…could have *lost* it, and killed her, over getting dumped."

Some kid.

Or some married man.

TEN

Sally and I had agreed to meet by the front entrance at eight, but I was a little late. My appointment with Mr. Jacobs had been the last slotted, and ran over some. I found her just outside, smoking. The sky still promised rain and it was cold, but if a kid wanted a cigarette, a kid did that outside.

"I hate to see you doing that," I said.

"What, smoking? Why?"

"It's a terrible thing to do to such a nice body."

"Aren't you sweet? How did it go?"

We walked arm-in-arm toward her Mustang. I filled her in, more or less, especially how both Candy and Roger got high marks from everyone I'd spoken to.

We were at her car. She leaned against the driver's-side door, blowing smoke at me impudently. I leaned on the vehicle behind me, a yellow Buick Turbo muscle car. Probably not a parent's car. Somebody young and dumb who dug speed and bad mileage.

Otherwise, few cars remained in the lot, two or three pulling out now, beams cutting the night. Parents, teachers, and kids had mostly gone home.

"I listened to some of it," she said.

"What do you mean?"

"Your meetings. I stood outside and eavesdropped, you know?"

"What did you do that for?"

"Because I'm a bad girl." She blew a smoke ring at me. "Didn't you know I was a bad girl?"

"I guessed."

"I heard you say you've been hanging around with Candy's Aunt Jenny."

"She's been helping."

She put an ugly smirk on her pretty face. "A Stockwell, helping clear *Roger*? Doubt it."

"Clarence and his boy Larry are the anti-Vale crowd. Jenny has an open mind."

"Jenny has an open everything. Did you fuck her?"

"Hey."

Her chin went up. "I loved Candy, but her aunt's a raging skank. What does she have that I don't have?"

"I didn't know it was an issue."

She tossed her cigarette with an unnerving confidence and crossed the small distance between us, and took one of my hands and placed it on a pert breast and grabbed my package in a firm but gentle if overflowing handful.

Her voice was a purr with claws behind it. "Who do you think taught Candy what's what?"

"Her aunt?"

She sneered and squeezed my balls a little, and it almost hurt, but my dick was rising to the occasion. She pressed her mouth to mine and she tasted sweet and smoky. We played tonsil hockey for a while, and she was stroking me through my pants, a gifted girl who could do at least two things at once.

This was ill-advised, but fun. I hadn't necked in a high school parking lot in a long time.

"*Hey!*"

My God, had the principal caught us?

A big guy in a yellow letter jacket with black sleeves came rushing at us, arms pumping like pistons. He'd been inside the school.

Enter Rod Pettibone.

Broad-shouldered, tiny-eyed Rod Pettibone, with short blond hair and a small nose and wide mouth over a shovel jaw. He looked like Moose in the *Archie* comics, but cartoonier.

"That's my friggin' car!" he yelled.

He was maybe ten yards from us.

And then he was ten feet away, saying, "And that's my friggin' *girl*!"

He came at me like he was rushing the line. I backed up and Sally plastered herself against her own car, taking herself out of the play, providing Rod the hole he needed to charge through and take his man down.

Which he did, a good two-hundred-twenty-some pounds of him smashing me onto my back into the cement, knocking every ounce of wind out of me. He climbed off and picked me up like a bag of laundry and flung me against the tail of the Mustang, my lower back taking the brunt. Sally, eyes showing white all around, had her hands up like a pretty hold-up victim.

Before I could recover, he hit me in the right side of the head, and my brain spun, then he gave me hard shots in the ribs, on either side, followed by a deep right fist in the pit of the stomach.

I doubled over and puked, which made him back away, not wanting to get anything on the letter jacket apparently, and that's when I kicked out and the heel of my shoe caught him in the right knee. Hard.

Fucking hard.

"My knee!" he screamed, going down on his other one. "Not my *knee*!"

"Good luck with your scholarship, jackass," I said gratuitously.

And passed out, grinning.

⚜

Thunder woke me.

We were moving through the night. I was in a car. Someone was driving. Sally. In the Mustang. Mustang Sally. High beams revealing a gravel road, walls of ghostly corn stalks at our sides. Sky a gray canopy of rolling, roiling clouds, shot through with sudden, brief veins of electricity.

More thunder.

She smiled over me, pretty little face in the midst of all that frizzy tawny-blonde hair, given an odd glow in the dashboard light. "You're awake."

"Head's swimming. What…what's going on?"

"I'm taking you home with me. You're my lost puppy, you know? You need some TLC."

"Not necessary."

"Rod knocked you out. But you got him back. The way he hobbled away, crying, you might have cost us the season."

"Kicked him."

"You did. He has kind of a bad knee anyway."

I blinked. Headache, migraine level. Nauseated. Sky with those dark moving clouds and crackling veins of lightning and the gravel road and the towering black walls of corn stalks, felt like I was moving through a dream. I leaned back. Seat was comfortable. Bucket seat. Comfortable, but Jesus my fucking head.

Somebody, not the girl, said, "I think it's a concussion. Mild concussion."

Man's voice.

Me.

"That's what I thought. Try not to swallow your tongue, okay?"

"Okay."

"I'm gonna watch you for a couple hours. I'll be Nurse Sally, you know? You'll be fine. Tender loving care. That's what TLC stands for."

"Does it?"

"Just relax. You need to rest. Nothing strenuous." She peeked over the steering wheel toward the sky. "Is it gonna snow or rain, I wonder? What do you think?"

"Not cold enough. Not snow. Rain."

And I either passed out again or fell asleep.

"Come on, big boy," she said.

She was helping me out of the car. I blinked myself awake, head still swimming but blurry vision gradually coming into focus. Girl had surprising strength, but then she was a dancer and a sort of athlete. She almost yanked me to my feet and slipped an arm around my waist, to guide me on my shaky legs up a sidewalk to a vague two-story structure where a short flight of wooden steps led to an open porch.

We made it up them somehow, as the sky roared and lightning flashed and illuminated the world, including this structure. A farmhouse, white clapboard, older, indifferently maintained. With an arm still around my waist, she opened the screen and worked a key in the front door.

Then we were inside. She did not turn on any lights, just walked me across a living room to a couch and deposited me there, putting two throw pillows behind my back. She unlaced my sneakers and removed them. Then she disappeared.

I lay in darkness and breathed deep. My head throbbed with pain but it no longer swam. I fell asleep again for a few moments or maybe minutes, but then was wakened by the sensation of cold pressing against the right side of my head.

"Ice," she said. She was more a presence than anything I could actually see in the dark room. "In a washcloth. Can you hold it there?"

"Yes."

"I'm gonna get you something."

"Okay."

She came back maybe a minute later with a glass of water and two small round yellow pills.

"Percodan," she said, helping me sit up. "Good shit. Drink the water down."

I did as I was told.

Thunder rumbled, lightning flashed, strobing through the edges around drawn curtains, making evident a very old-fashioned room around me.

Still holding the cloth-wrapped ice to my head, I asked, "Is your aunt here?"

"No," she said.

"She doesn't have a very comfortable couch."

She giggled. "No, she doesn't. It's really old. Do you think you could make it up some stairs?"

"Think so."

"We'll get you into bed."

"Okay."

The vague outline of her drifted away, then a floor lamp snapped on and an under-furnished living room took shape. Very sparse, '30s and '40s crap, like an older person might have, or someone who shopped at Goodwill. Beyond was a dining room with a table but not much else, and an old kitchen past that.

She got me to my feet, dispensed with the ice. I breathed deep some more, and allowed her to walk me around to where the stairs to the upstairs were opposite the front door. They were narrow and I told her I could make it on my own. She let me try, and with the help of the banister, I managed.

A single dim light was on at the top. Again, it revealed very sparse furnishings, and old wallpaper, peeling a little. She walked me into a darkened room, but the meager light from the hall indicated a bed. Jesus, another fucking waterbed. Round.

Black sheets. Did all the females in goddamn fucking Stockwell have waterbeds?

Outside the sky rumbled an inconclusive answer.

The rest of the bedroom seemed vague, but I could tell posters were on the walls, and judging by the waterbed, this was hardly the aunt's room. And it was not a small space, more a master bedroom than what a teenage girl, living with an older relative, might have. That was just my sense of it, though—she didn't turn on a light.

She asked, "You want help with your clothes?"

"I can sleep in them."

"No, let's get them off you. That heavy coat anyway."

She did that, then went ahead and tugged off my shirt and tie, and undid my pants, and I stepped out of them. She guided me in my shorts to the nearby bed and I got under the sheets. The waterbed was warm, heated, and the gentle movement of it was soothing. Maybe waterbeds were okay. Maybe they were the shit.

I fell asleep.

The sky exploded in an artillery barrage that gave me just a brief Vietnam flashback as I sat up in bed, a little thrown by its waterlogged instability, and heard the rain finally break loose. There was a lot of it. Driving. Hammering. Machine-gunning.

Somebody was in bed next to me.

"You awake?" Sally asked.

"Yeah."

"How do you feel?"

"Okay. Better. All right."

"It's really coming down. You were right, Jack. *Not* snow. If it was, we'd be up to our butts in it, you know?"

"Yeah. Uh, Sally. Thanks for helping me."

"No problem."

No thunder now. Just driving rain, pummeling the roof.

"That kid hit me with a shovel, I swear."

"Rod's really strong. I yelled at him for what he did to you. I told him we were through."

"Are you?"

"Yeah. He's not very smart. He's a terrible fucking lay."

"Why go with him?"

I sensed more than saw her shrug, and she said, "He was Candy's guy. It's a status thing, you know?"

"Where's your aunt?"

"Not here."

"But where is she? Elderly aunt of yours?"

Drumming rain filled the silence that followed.

Then she said: "How are you at keeping secrets?"

"Not bad. Pretty good."

"…My aunt doesn't live here."

"Where *does* she live?"

"She lives in California and she's only in her thirties, and she doesn't give a fucking shit about me."

"That's not her furniture downstairs."

"No, that's…that's just junk I picked up. For if somebody from the school comes around. Actually, it's a pretense I don't need to keep up anymore. I'm eighteen. You can be on your own at eighteen."

"But when you moved here, you weren't eighteen."

"No. Sixteen. My parents died in a small plane crash outside San Francisco. They had some money that went to his brother and her sister, my aunt. But they had a decent insurance policy, and it went right to me. The courts gave my aunt responsibility for me, and we lived in Santa Barbara. But my aunt's husband —husband number three, I think—he had the hots for me. She kind of kicked me out."

"That was harsh."

"Not really. I kind of…fucked him, you know? Not fucked him over, I mean…you know, actually fucked him one afternoon."

"Ah."

"I inherited a couple of other things from my folks, including this farmhouse. Actually, there's a farm that goes with it, but I rent it out. Or my aunt does."

"Is this an imaginary aunt?"

"No, the real one out in California. She was all for me getting my ass out of there, and fine with my plan to live by myself. Any help I needed to fool the school in Stockwell, she was up for. Better them than her."

"You mean, the administrators at Stockwell High think you live out here with your aunt? An elderly aunt, based on the way you furnished the downstairs."

"Right. That's why this was my first parent–teacher night, you know? Pretty slick for a kid, huh? Pretty cool? Now I guess maybe I'm keeping up the false front more out of habit than anything else. And maybe I'd still get in trouble, even though I am, like, eighteen."

Was the rain letting up, just a little?

"Sally, you're a girl of great initiative."

"Thanks."

"Is this why you didn't go out for the pageants, like all the other Stockwell girls?"

"Yeah. Really, I'd love to. They're stupid, pageants, but I could pull that off. I could ace it."

"I know you could. Who all knows your secret?"

"Well, Roger does. He's my best friend. Or is now that Candy's gone. She knew all about it. She knew everything. She used to come out here and we would have such a blast. Getting high. Getting wasted."

"Big parties out here?"

"Oh no. Just Candy and me. If I had a big blow-out out here, you think my secret would be safe for long? Not fuckin' hardly!"

"Sally…did you ever consider that Candy saw how you'd remade your life, and maybe she tried to do the same thing with hers? She and her father had really bottomed out, after all, and—"

She turned, moving closer to me. The scent of Charlie perfume tickled my nostrils.

Hope in her voice, she asked, "So you think Candy might be out there somewhere? Alive? Maybe tearing it up in some dinner theater or somewhere? Some little club? Wouldn't it be a hoot if she were stripping or something! She had the body for it. *Has* the body for it. Gotta stay positive."

"You really think she might be, Sally? Out there somewhere?"

The rain was just pattering now, but you could hear the thunder complaining again, only distant.

"No.…What I really think is, she would *never* run away. And if she did? She'd tell me. We were tight. Really, really tight."

"Then what *did* happen to her?"

"Some perv did it. Maybe even Rod."

"You said he was a pussycat."

"Yeah, but…really, cats are pretty mean, when you get right down to it. He's got a temper."

"You're telling me."

"*You* tell *me*—are you feeling better? How bad are you hurting?"

"I'm okay. My ribs hurt. I hope he didn't crack them."

"Let me get something."

The waterbed sloshed as she climbed down and opened the door and, before she scurried into the hall where the light was still on, gave me a glimpse of her mostly naked shape, small, curvy, her dimpled, high-cheeked bottom barely hidden by pink lacy panties.

When she returned, she clicked on a little lamp on a boxy modern nightstand. She'd brought a tube of Metholatum ointment. She sat cross-legged on the unstable bed and rubbed the stuff into the areas around my sore ribs; the burning sensation helped, maybe because it was a distraction. Her bare, pert breasts definitely were. You will be proud of me: I did not stare.

Instead, I took stock of my surroundings. This did appear to be a master bedroom, at least the farmhouse variety, though it was definitely Sally's bedroom. Only the downstairs carried the pretense of some older person living here. This looked like a coed's dream dorm room.

The rectangular space bore old-fashioned wallpaper that was mostly obscured—opposite the waterbed, for example, was a massive projection television. Down at left stood a pair of tall, narrow white bookcases, joined above by a long single shelf with sideways-stacked speaker cabinets. The shelves bore no books but plenty of LPs, audio cassettes, and prerecorded VHS tapes, plus a top-end sound system with turntable.

Between the bookcases, underneath the shelf that joined them, a trio of black light posters (Jimi Hendrix, Vanilla Fudge, Janis Joplin) floated over a black leather sofa. A low-lying glass coffee table in front of the sofa perched on a multi-colored throw rug on the polished wood floor. A wall of mirrored closet doors was at my right.

"Better?" she asked, returning the cap to the tube.

"Better."

"I should wash my hands."

She ran off to do that and I sat up straighter in bed, propping a black pillowcased pillow behind me. My headache had been knocked back by the Percodan, and I really did feel pretty good, suddenly wide awake. A little round metal nightstand clock said 11:30 P.M. I should get back to my Holiday Inn bed.

When the bare-breasted pixie returned, I said, "I hate to impose, but maybe you should run me home. This *is* a school night."

"Why, since when do you go to Stockwell High?"

"You know what I mean, Sally."

"You're feeling better?"

"Quite a bit, thanks."

She sat on the edge of the bed and it bounced in its sloshing way. Her grin was cute and a little feral, the babyish upper lip pulled back over small white teeth. "You up for some fun?"

"Maybe not. Probably not up to it."

"Come on, couldn't we have some fun?" She hopped off the bed. "What if I just dance for you, and see if you're…up to it?"

"Dance."

"Yeah. Wait here. I want to put on some special makeup."

But before she left, she shimmied out of the pink panties. And I'll be damned if she wasn't bare down there, shaved or I don't what—it was startling. I'd never seen a female so Barbie Doll hairless, disturbing, too, because she was so petite and young. It was enough to make my dick sit up and shake its head, like it couldn't believe what it was seeing.

And what the fuck kind of makeup, I thought, *requires a girl taking off her panties?*

When she returned, four or five minutes later, she didn't seem to have any more makeup on than before. She was still naked, as she walked over to the shelves with the sound system and picked out a homemade cassette tape and inserted it into the machine. "Smoke on the Water" by Deep Purple burst out of the speakers like the thunder had returned.

Then she cranked it some more.

She asked, almost shouting, "Could you switch off the bed-side lamp?"

I said I could, and did.

"Can you watch me from there?" she yelled sweetly. "Does it hurt? I'm gonna work it over here."

I swung my body around, ribs complaining just a little, but the hell with them. Though darkness had returned, I could tell she was moving the coffee table to one side and making a little performance area out of the throw rug.

Then she went over to a nearby wall switch and a click announced overhead black-light tubing coming on to make Jimi and the Fudge and Janis glow. Also her lips and her finger- and toenails and the tips of her breasts and the petals of flesh between her legs—all glowing red as she did a swaying dance to the thumping music, arms waving, feet shifting weight from leg to leg, the mirrored wall behind me echoing and multi- plying her. Then she began to twist and grind in rhythm with the pounding guitar riff, *bamp bamp BAH, bamp bamp BAH bah,* a native dance that grew in intensity, lifting right fist and left knee, then left fist and right knee, swinging her arms, her torso, awkward, graceful, until finally she tossed herself on the couch on her back and spread her legs and her pussy glowed red and so did the tips of her little bobbling breasts, and the red fingertips of her upturned palms, tickled the air, summoned me.

I climbed out of bed like a starving man to a meal and there was no thought of protection, no thought of anything rational, just the center of her sex demanding my attention. I climbed on top of her, where she nestled in the V of the sofa, falling between her splayed legs, plunging into her, and she writhed and did her savage bump-and-grind as my head throbbed from concussion and my dick throbbed from the hot tight wetness of her teenage snatch, and there was no love in it, no emotion, no passion, just lust, and she laughed while I pounded her, driving myself into her, like I wanted to kill her with it, but finally she won, laughing in savage orgasm, as it bled seed into that red gaping wound.

ELEVEN

The late morning was sunny and clear, probably seventy degrees, last night's heavy rain a shimmering mild memory of scattered puddles around Stockwell Park. Plump green pines lorded it over trees largely bereft of leaves, spectators on the periphery of the rough terrain that rose through rock outcroppings to a cliff-like bluff.

Jenny, seated across the picnic table from me, a Colonel Sanders thigh in her hands, said, "If this Indian summer weather keeps up, it'll get crazy out here this weekend."

"Even during the off-season?"

She nodded, rolled the light-green eyes. "The locals *love* having the park to themselves, and with one last gasp of not shitty weather? Crazy, I tell ya."

I glanced around at the aberrational paradise in the midst of Missouri mediocrity. "Surprised it's not a state park."

"It belonged to the Stockwell family, you will not be surprised to learn. My ancestors very generously gave it to the city in 1905. Maybe they'd have held onto it, if they knew buggy whips would be going belly up."

We had walked here from a graveled parking lot, through a wooded area, fallen leaves crackling underfoot, and across an antiquated but sturdy wooden bridge, of width enough for a buggy maybe but not a car, over a clear, sand-bottomed stream.

Now we were seated at one of half a dozen picnic tables in the flat area at the foot of rising rocky terrain with various rustic signs pointing to this foot trail or that, with advice attached:

"Great for Beginners," "Seasoned Hikers Only," and so on. Brick outdoor grills were here and there, and a covered shelter.

"Big family spot in the summer, huh?" I observed pointlessly. No jacket today, just sweatshirt and jeans.

She nodded, chewed, then said, "Sure, but the real draw is college kids—this is a big spring break area for campers and hikers. Quiet trails, incredible views. Birds to watch, quiet places to just get away and enjoy nature."

I was bird-watching, too—a full-breasted thrush called Jenny Stockwell, who despite gold hoop earrings in the nest of black curls looked less gypsy today and more earth mother. She looked pleasantly funky in rust-color sweater and acid-wash jeans, with almost no makeup, just a hint of pink lipstick. The sun revealed lines in her face, like cracks in fine china.

Just this morning I'd been shaken awake by a barely legal Lolita urging me to hurry up ("Come on, come on, move your ass—don't make me late to fucking home room!"). I'd moved my ass, and fortunately Sally had passed right by the Holiday Inn on her way to school, making dropping me off "no biggie."

Miss Meadows was the compliant, sexually voracious teenage vixen that every man thought he wanted. But somehow I came away from that exhausting "trippy" night grateful for the fun ride but with a new appreciation for Jenny Stockwell's mature charms.

Of course, since Jenny's mature charms included blow jobs between garbage cans behind dives, I should perhaps not be lauded for my Alan Alda-like sensitivity.

I'd called and said I wanted to take her out for lunch, and Jenny suggested "a sort of a picnic," since maybe I'd like a glimpse at the part of Stockwell that made it Missouri's Little Vacationland. So I'd picked her up at home, thinking she had plenty of woods right around there to satisfy any rustic urge I might have, but I was just too damn polite to say so. We went through the Kentucky Fried Chicken drive-through and were ready to rough it.

The translucent green eyes studied me like something on a slide. "This isn't just a luncheon date, is it?"

"Sometimes a chicken breast is just a chicken breast, Ms. Freud."

"Not with you. Never with you, Jack. Always something brewing upstairs. What were you up to last night?"

I chewed chicken breast. "I went to parent–teacher night with Sally Meadows."

"Ha! That little slut. Well, she was Candy's best friend, so that makes sense. Did you get laid?"

"Of course I didn't get laid. She's just a high school kid. What kind of animal do you take me for?"

"You really want me to answer?"

I dropped the breast onto crackling paper and looked right at her. "All right, then. She took me back to her teenage pad and stripped down and turned on the black light and danced for me, with her privates all aglow."

"Shut-up, you goof."

"There's more. She put on Deep Purple. 'Smoke on the Water.' Pranced like a cross between a stripteaser and a Zulu mating dance. You should've seen it. Might've given you some ideas for a painting."

She was laughing now, at my zany display of wit. "Will you stop it? What did you *really* do?"

I shrugged. "Well, Sally is Mr. Roger's favorite little protégée. I approached her, said I wanted to clear his name in my article, and she helped me talk to some teachers."

"Teachers who told you what?"

I shrugged again. "They all whitewashed him."

"That doesn't make him innocent."

"No. But what I learned convinces me there are plenty of other candidates for Candy's murderer out there, besides a gay dance instructor. That Pettibone kid, for example. I had a little dust-up with him."

She looked mildly alarmed. "What happened?"

"I was just standing talking to Sally in the school parking lot, when he took a run at me like I'd been making out with her or something." I told her the rest of it fairly straight, even showed her my bruised sides.

"You're lucky he didn't kill you," she said, with a shudder, as I tugged down my sweatshirt.

"Which makes my point. And God knows how many other boys and men got a taste of Candy, and didn't like being denied later on."

She was eating her coleslaw, lackadaisically. "I suppose that's true. But I don't think you'll ever convince Daddy. Or Larry, either. All they can see is Roger Vale."

"You're probably right."

Then she dropped her spork and leaned in excitedly, green eyes urgent. "But maybe *you* could find out. Maybe you can keep at this, stay at it—I could underwrite your effort, if need be."

"What?"

She shrugged and gypsy curls danced and the hoop earrings swung. "I know you probably can't afford to keep working on this story forever, not on spec. But what if you had the freedom to really stay and dig in? I could hire you to do that."

"And…do what exactly?"

"*Really* explore these suspects. The Pettibone boy, for instance. You said it yesterday, to Larry—if the spurned boyfriend killed Candy in a jealous rage, his father may have helped him cover up."

She didn't understand that I didn't really give a damn who killed Candy. I wasn't looking for a murderer, not really. My job was to kill whoever it was that wanted *Vale* dead. The person or persons who had wrongly targeted the dance instructor.

In addition to which, I was coming to the end here in Stockwell. I really liked Jenny. We may have met in less than storybook fashion, but a part of me wished I really could marry her and settle down here in Norman Rockwell-ville. She was rich. She looked great. She was smart. And she was hot in the sack. What was not to love?

But that scenario would only have played out if I were really a journalist researching a story for the *St. Louis Sun*. And if I wasn't a semi-retired hitman who had in the last several days smothered one killer with a pillow and slit another one's throat before stuffing him in his car trunk.

Somebody, somewhere, would be learning soon, if they hadn't already, that the team sent to kill Roger Vale had failed before they started. And more than just that, had been taken rudely out of the game.

So I played a different card.

"Jenny," I said, nodding, "that's a real possibility, me staying here...of course, I could never accept your money."

Sure I could.

"You're sweet, Jack, but I *insist*—"

I raised a palm. Somewhere an owl hooted, its "who?" indicating that somebody around here, anyway, had doubts about me.

"While I was out sniffing around," I said, "and *not* just at that parent–teacher conference...I picked up on a nasty rumor."

She sat up. "Really? What?"

"I can only share it with you if you promise not to repeat it—not to anyone."

"Well, Jack, of course."

"You'll be tempted."

She showed me that beautiful, just slightly tobacco-stained smile. "I hope by now you know you can trust me."

It was way too early in our relationship, if that's what this was, for that to be true.

But I said, "Of course. Only there's also a second condition."

"All right. Go on."

I leaned in conspiratorially. "You can't ask me where or how I heard this. Promise?"

"Promise. I promise."

Very quietly, as if we were sitting in a crowded restaurant and not in an outdoor cathedral at a picnic table among five other such empty tables, I said, "Somebody may have taken a contract out on Roger Vale."

She reared back. "Contract? What?"

"You heard me, Jenny. Someone may have paid to have him killed."

She was shaking her head, earrings having none of it. "No, that kind of thing just doesn't happen. Not in real life."

"Sure it does. People kill people for money all the time. But this isn't an unhappy hubby in a bar, handing a shady character fifty bucks to kill the missus. This is…it *appears* to be…something, well, higher up the food chain."

Still shaking her head, but more slowly, she said, "I don't follow…."

"A contract killing is expensive, Jen. And something not just anyone can afford, much less arrange. Someone may…I haven't confirmed this, it's rumor, understand…*may* have paid a considerable amount of money to bring in a professional killer."

Halfway through that she had begun shaking her head again. "No, that's crazy. No. Just impossible. This is Stockwell, Jack. Small-town Stockwell, Missouri, remember? That kind of thing just—"

"No, it happens. Just like pretty high school girls sometimes get kidnapped and defiled and murdered."

She was frowning—frightened and irritated. "Why tell me this? What can I do about it?"

"You heard your father say that he didn't want my help. He didn't want a newspaper's help. That he has...how did he put it? 'The situation in hand.' "

She swallowed, nodded. "He said that. He did say that."

"Okay, then." I reached past our respective half-eaten plates and took her hand. "Stay calm. We're just talking, here, okay? This is small-town Stockwell, I get that, but your family is very wealthy. Is there anything in the past that might connect your father to...don't freak out on me now...organized crime? You know—Mafia. The mob."

She laughed, a little hysteria around the edges. She drew her hand away, getting ready to light up a Camel. "Now you're so far out there, it's ridiculous. There's nothing...."

And then she frowned, the unlit cigarette hanging off her lower lip impotently.

"What?" I asked.

She fired up the Camel with her lighter, took a deep draw, expelled blue smoke, eyes narrowing. "Well...years ago, there was a dog track here. Must have been the twenties, early thirties. There was gambling. I don't know if it was legal or not, but...I do remember hearing that Daddy had partners from Chicago in that track."

That would do it.

She went on: "I don't think it lasted long—maybe eight or ten years? It was turned into a stock-car track for a while. I think that closed in the early seventies."

"I asked you about this Mafia possibility," I said gently, "because that's how, *where*, someone like your father or your brother might be able to hire that kind of—"

"*Not* my brother," she said, shaking her head so hard the hoop earrings damn near flew off. "That's *not* Larry. He wouldn't be a part of anything illegal or…violent."

"He threatened to strangle Vale."

She batted the air. "Come on, Jack. That's just a father out of his mind with grief talking."

"What about *your* father?"

"Oh," she said, unhesitatingly, "in his case? Credible. Highly credible."

"Really?"

"Really. He loved his granddaughter. And he's an old man. He doesn't want to go to his grave without seeing Candy's killer brought to justice. I buy it entirely. Never mind that we don't even know for sure that she's dead." She shivered, though the sun was still warm.

"There may be another concern.…"

Her eyes rolled. "Jesus fucking Christ, what *else* is there?"

I spoke as if this were all just occurring to me. "If *I* heard this rumor, then the *real* killer…as you say, if there *is* a killer… may have heard it, too. *Vale* may have heard it. And even if your father is innocent in this—and it *is* just a wild rumor—he could be in danger."

All this enormous bullshit brought forth a tiny smile from her. "My father? In danger? Hard to imagine."

"Why? Does he live in a fortress?"

She laughed a huff of smoke. "No. It's just hard thinking of anything…*touching* him. He'll be eighty next year, and he hasn't spent a night in the hospital since he had his tonsils out as a kid. Except for when we kids were born, and when Mom died. He still has an office in the bank building, and keeps regular nine-to-five hours. He's a brick. He *does* live in a big house… but alone."

I frowned. "A man of his position surely he has a live-in cook and housekeeper…?"

"He has a cook-housekeeper, but not live-in."

"Then he must have a security staff."

"No. A security system, but he never turns it on when he's home. He's often up and down all night. Goes to bed at eight, sleeps a while, then rises, wide awake again at one or two and reads in his study, then maybe back in bed at four."

"Oh. So then his security system is motion-activated, something he only turns on when he leaves the house."

"Right. Do you *really* think he's in danger?"

I sighed. Pretended to think her question over. "Probably not. If your father were to meet with foul play, that would only confirm what he'd said about Candy's murder, and for that matter Vale. The investigation that followed would be so extensive that…no, I shouldn't have mentioned that. He's safe enough."

Tension seemed drain out of her. "Thank you for saying that. I hope it's true." She swallowed, frowned, stubbed her cigarette out on the picnic table. "Because I don't know if I could handle another…another family tragedy."

"Yeah," I said. "That would be terrible."

After lunch, she walked me up a path that began gentle and got quickly steep. Before it turned into anything treacherous, she led me through two high sandstone ledges to a small log cabin nestled among some pines.

"During the season," she said, gesturing toward the idyllic-looking structure, "my family pays for a ranger to be on duty. Just something nice to do for the town."

"Ah."

"It's vacant now. I have a key. There's usually some beer in the little fridge. Would you like one?"

"I wouldn't mind. Five minutes of hiking really takes it out of a guy."

She laughed gently and took me by the hand.

The interior was just one big room, with a desk, some file cabinets, a floor heater, a small restroom, and a single bed covered in a red-and-black plaid blanket. Also, the promised fridge with several bottles of Olympia. I got out two bottles and opened them for us.

She sat on the bed and patted the spot next to her. I took it.

"Can't you please stay?" she asked, her expression painfully earnest. "And work on your story? If you could crack this case, think of what it could mean. To your career. To me, and my family."

I sipped the beer. "I hope you didn't bring me here to try to bribe me."

She smiled a little. The lines in her face only made her prettier. "What would it take?"

"Nothing would work. I'm too principled."

She pulled off the red sweater. No bra. Probably the implants made that unnecessary. I kissed her breasts. I kissed her neck. I kissed her lips. She kicked off her sneakers. Tugged off her jeans. Nothing under them but bush. She was a nude woman in white socks.

"Jack...nothing fancy...not in the mood...just missionary style, okay? Like two old married people...."

I got out of the rest of my clothes, and I used a rubber though I don't think she cared, but I had been stupid last night and maybe caught something off that wild little teen, and I wouldn't want to hurt Jenny any more than I already was going to.

So we made love, and it was lovemaking, not fucking, and that was the difference with a real woman, as opposed to some silly girl, wasn't it? This was a woman whose emotion was deeper than the part of her I was plunging into, again and again, sunlight streaming through pines and a filmy curtain, giving her a glow that didn't require fucking black light.

Nothing fancy.

So much better than fancy.

Around three o'clock, following my phone call, Roger Vale let me in the stage entry of his dance studio. Already in the black tights for tonight's class, he led me to the steps at the side of the stage that led down into the auditorium, where we took seats next to each other in the first row.

"Yesterday," I said, catching him up, "the surveillance guy showed back up. I've taken care of him."

Dark eyes flashed in the narrow fake-tan handsome face. "My God, how? When? *Where?*"

"Goddamnit, you do not need to know that. You don't need to know *any* of it. It's bad for you if you do."

"Sorry. Sorry."

"Yeah." I sat back, shrugged. "Didn't mean to snap at you, Roger. It's just that time is getting critical. The surveillance guy coming back to check on his partner, that could mean whoever they're working for may know something went wrong."

"The person who hired them, you mean?" He nervously stroked his mustache with a thumbnail.

"Possibly. More likely a broker they work through, a middleman. It just means that I…*we*…have to act very soon. Actually, today, if possible. Tonight."

While his forehead and eyes frowned, his mouth formed a small smile. "You mean…you *know*? You know who hired this awful thing—for certain?"

"That's the problem. It's not for certain."

"No?"

"Roger, I'm not the police—I don't have a forensics lab. I don't have computers. And I sure as hell don't have the luxury of conducting a full-scale, leisurely investigation."

He risked another little smile. "Sally says you did well at the school last night."

"In the sense that it became clear there are plenty of better suspects than you in this thing, yes. But somebody doesn't give a damn. Somebody took that contract out, anyway."

His eyes flared. "Who, damnit? Who do you think did this?"

"The same person who you've suspected from the start—the old man, the family patriarch, Clarence Stockwell. The only other possibility is the girl's father—Lawrence. But he's just too weak a sister. It *has* to be the father."

"What about the other Stockwell?"

"What other Stockwell?"

"The aunt! The sister who *isn't* weak! She and Candy were close. You said you'd talked to her."

I nodded. "Yes, and she's your only rooting section. She doesn't suspect you at all."

"But…couldn't she be *playing* you? She's got a reputation as a wild character around town."

"I suppose she could be playing me. You never know in a situation like this. Which is why you have a decision to make, Roger. Not an easy one."

He frowned, narrowed his eyes, cocked his head, His Master's Voice. "…Okay."

"I would give it ninety-five percent that Old Man Stockwell is behind this. All by his lonesome. That taking him out will make you no longer a target."

"Even though he's already put it in motion?"

"The team sent to take you out is dead. Once *Clarence* is dead, the contract is dead, too. If there was a final payment due, who would pay it? No. You'll be free and clear."

He frowned again, a deep groove forming between the heavy eyebrows. "But you say there's a five percent chance that—"

"Roger, I just pulled that number out of my ass. It could be higher, it could be lower. That's why you may prefer to send me on my way. Without paying me another red cent. Which is only right. I haven't delivered. I'm cool with that."

"Take my chances...I don't understand...."

I sighed. "The team Old Man Stockwell hired didn't deliver. They in fact wound up toast. That may be enough to discourage the old man from trying again. Might even be enough to discourage that middleman from sending another team. *Might*."

"Might," Vale said hollowly.

"The question is, are you okay with me removing the old boy? Strictly on the circumstantial evidence I've been able to gather? I could try to get a confession out of him, before I drop the hammer, but that could get messy. And I would frankly have to ask for more money. Say, another five thousand."

"*Stop* it! You're making my head spin...."

"I will stop. Right now I'll stop."

He looked like he might cry. "Good."

"All I need from you is that decision. Are we both comfortable taking out the old man? Do we feel confident enough that this solves the problem to go ahead with it?"

"What's your opinion?"

"You know my opinion. He hired it. No question in my mind. But if there's a question in *yours*, then I'm out of here."

Vale's eyes were moving; his hands were chest high, fists opening and closing, clenching, unclenching.

"Do it," he said finally. "He's made my life miserable. Fucking *do* it, Quarry."

"No problem," I said. "I'm going to make a move tonight, but just in case I have to abort, you keep your head inside this concrete bunker till you hear from me. Should be tonight. Could be two days. It'll be by phone. Till then, just keep your head the hell in."

"What about an alibi? You said I should have an alibi."

"Get Sally to come stay here. You *are* aware she's living alone, right? No real aunt out there?"

"I am," he admitted.

"Okay then. Neither of you stick your damn heads out."

"Understood," he said. The normally half-hooded eyes were wide. "And, Quarry? I do thank you for laying it all out like this. You might have come around and said, 'It's the old man,' and I'd have said 'Fine,' and you could have done it and gone. Instead, you showed real integrity."

"No thanks necessary," I said, getting up, shrugging. "You know how it is. I'm a professional."

TWELVE

Clarence Stockwell lived, apparently alone, in a near mansion at the crest of a rise, with the downward slope of his backyard adjacent to the ninth hole of the Stockwell Golf & Country Club's eighteen-hole course. According to a squib in the latest issue of *Stockwell Living* (complimentary to Holiday Inn guests), the "showplace" had been built on the site of the old clubhouse; twenty years ago, the nine-hole course had been expanded to eighteen, and the "new" clubhouse (likely paid for by Stockwell, too) was a mile down Country Club Lane.

The two-story beige-brick structure with black shutters and roof, a late '6os take on French Provincial, might have been a small, exclusive hotel. The front entrance, its black wrought-iron door guarded by black urns, had an overhang with pillars; two cherubs on pedestals guarded the sloping lawn. The circular drive had an offshoot around right to a three-car garage that faced the side street, taking up most of a one-story addition; that and a similar but smaller annex on the other side hugged the house like irregular bookends.

This impressive but not obnoxious rich man's mini-manse was on the northwest side of town—not far from the park where Stockwell's daughter and I shared Kentucky Fried Chicken—perched on the corner of Country Club Lane and Park View Avenue. This was a residential area running to expensive homes built in the teens or twenties; Clarence's castle, on the former country club site, seemed strikingly more new than its neighbors, and just enough bigger to make its point.

My stakeout began around quarter to five, dusk having already given in to evening. I'd gone from the dance studio back to the Holiday Inn, to collect the nine millimeter and snubnose .38, and to change into the white shirt, skinny brown tie and brown slacks I'd worn in journalist mode.

That glimpse of propriety under my fleece-lined jacket might make me less conspicuous in this upscale neighborhood. Even if I was sitting in a Pinto. Next time I wouldn't be such a damn cheapskate.

I was parked across the way, just slightly down Park View, when a silver-gray black-vinyl-roof Town Car rolled into and up the circular drive. No one else in the big car, just Clarence Stockwell himself at the wheel—no sissy move like using a chauffeur for him—who swung the Lincoln around, raised a garage door with a remote, and sealed himself within. Jenny said her father worked regular hours, nine to five, and it was five-fifteen. That seemed right.

At five-thirty, I had just moved the car to a position on Country Club Lane when a black woman in her fifties in a cloth coat and a headscarf emerged from a door alongside the triple garage doors. The second non-white I'd seen in Stockwell. She walked to a vehicle parked off to the right, a '70s piece of shit Buick. Like I could talk, in my Pinto.

This would be the housekeeper-cook. She had stayed just long enough to report to her boss that her work was done and a meal she'd prepared was warm and ready. Hers had been the only car parked on the cement apron. Unless someone else with garage privileges was already in that house, Clarence was alone in there.

Five minutes after the help departed, I got out and trotted across the street onto the golf course. The flag of the ninth hole was near enough that I could hear it flapping, but I couldn't see it. The night was breezy, dark and cold, my breath visible. By late afternoon, dark clouds had said, *Enough of this Indian summer shit*, and rolled back in to take over; a fairly good-size moon would be up under there somewhere, but no visible evidence supported that theory.

At least the sky wasn't grumbling tonight. If it exploded, though, we'd get snow this time, and what remained of yesterday's rain was ice now, little patches of it here and there, my sneakers crunching on occasion as I stayed low and made for the house.

Where the golf course ended and Stockwell's back yard began was a slope up to a flat area, much of it consumed by a private putting green and a patio, no lawn furniture out this time of year, not even a cherub standing guard. I knelt by a bush and studied the place. The big house was dark but for one room, the kitchen, right there on the first floor, near the garage.

That's why the rich are rich, my old man used to advise me; *they turn off the goddamn lights when they don't need them.*

Well, maybe that helped them stay rich, but I doubted it *made* them rich. And if I were rich, I would eat better than Clarence was tonight. You could see him through a many-paned window framed by black shutters, sitting by himself at a black, metal-legged table. He had taken off his gray suit coat and draped it over the back of his kitchen chair; now that he was home relaxing, he had gone wild and loosened his necktie.

He was eating the meal the colored girl (as he likely thought of the middle-aged woman) had prepared for him, maybe even serving him up before she left. The biggest man in Stockwell, Mr. Stockwell Himself, slurping soup, and what was that he was nibbling between spoonfuls? A grilled cheese sandwich. Occasionally sipping a glass of milk, too.

I drew closer. Stood right there at the edge of the window and watched him eat in a big white kitchen with a late '60s look.

His wife would have long since remodeled, if she hadn't died ten years ago. He was reading *Sports Illustrated*, apparently plucked from a pile of nearby mail—presumably he read *Forbes* and *BusinessWeek* and such at his office.

The soup seemed to be tomato. I hadn't had tomato soup and grilled cheese with a glass of milk for supper since I was home sick from junior high. And at the time, I'd had no idea I was eating like a multi-millionaire.

So easy. I could shoot him from here, so easy. Just take the nine mil from my jacket pocket, take aim, and I would be the wealthier of the two of us, since dead guys don't own shit.

Why didn't I?

There's a right way and a wrong way, and this was right enough to get the job done. Okay, maybe better to go in and stage a suicide and not just leave a flat-out murder, which would at the very least get my client called in for questioning.

But for me to find a locked door to deal with, and go in there and face him down, that was just wrong. Made no sense. Not when he was served up to me here, like soup and sandwich, framed in that window, like the target he was.

Then why didn't I get it fucking over with?

Not that long ago I would have. If you think I was getting soft, if you think I was hesitant because I liked this man's daughter, and there was a trickle of treacle running through the gristle that made up most of me, you are wrong. Or at least mostly you are. How had the Monkees put it? Was I a little bit wrong? And are you a little bit right?

But I wasn't just a guy who killed people now. I had turned into someone who actually had curiosity between his ears, who had to think about things besides the pattern of a target and what weapon to use and means of entrance and egress, from a house, from a city. I wasn't just killing people anymore. I had put myself in the position of having to think about the reasons why people were killed, before doing any killing myself (removing the lowlife likes of Farrell and Mateski excluded).

And something about this whole set-up was wrong.

Should I care? I had been paid money, and I would be paid more money. Maybe not enough to someday sit alone in a great big house and eat my soup and grilled cheese, but enough to pay the freight for a while. *He was sitting right there.* Almost facing me, angled to my right enough to make it unlikely he'd even notice when I took a single step to my left and fired.

But I didn't take out the nine mil. I compromised. I left the automatic in my pocket, though my hand was in there with it, clutching it, as with my left fist I knocked on that side door where the help had exited.

He ignored it at first. He was old enough to be hard of hearing, but I hadn't seen a hearing aid and somehow the man Jenny had described as a brick didn't seem likely to allow himself to go through life not hearing the world around him. No, he could hear, all right. He wasn't even wearing glasses as he read his magazine. He was a goddamn freak of nature.

I knocked again, pounding this time.

I kept it up, and finally the door opened about three inches, and an irritated slice of the big man's sharp-featured face glowered at me. "No deliveries after dark."

The door started to close and I managed to nose the toe of my left shoe in and say, "I'm sorry to bother you while you're eating, sir."

He frowned. His hair was silver and combed straight back— thinning from age, not going bald; he lacked his son's fashionable sideburns. "You...you're that...friend of my daughter's, aren't you? The reporter. You've already been told."

"Sir...I need a few minutes. It's important."

Red climbed into the grooved face and the dark eyes fixed on me like gun sights, as he opened the door wider. "I don't have a very high opinion of the press, young man, but I have an even lower one of rude people who bother other people at home. I went to college with the publisher of the *Sun*, and I can assure you, you will not have any luck placing any story there, not on this subject, not on any subject. Now, young man—go away."

He began to shut the door and I said, "The two men you hired to kill Roger Vale are dead. Interested in the details?"

That froze him. His eyes widened and lost their focus, his mouth yawned in the kind of stupidity that even the most brilliant person can feel, when he sees a car is about to hit him.

"If I wanted to kill you, sir, you'd be dead. There's a nine millimeter Browning automatic pointing at you right now. In my jacket pocket. And just moments ago, I could have dropped you face-down into your tomato soup. I'm coming in."

He backed up.

I shut the door behind me. We were in a hallway that at left opened up into a laundry room off of which was a door to the garage.

I asked, "Is there anyone else in the house?"

"Who are you? Your name isn't really Quarry, is it?"

"It will do." I showed him the nine mil. "Anyone else in the house?"

"No. I live alone. No live-in help."

"No one's coming over this evening? Your son maybe? Your daughter?"

His frown deepened. "No. You saw I was eating a quiet supper. I had nothing planned."

"Good. You're about to schedule me in. Let's get out of this entryway."

His expression was morose. He had aged ten years in the last two minutes. Of course that only made him look his real age.

He turned and moved slowly toward the kitchen, maybe half a dozen steps away; he was two or three inches taller than me, and outweighed me twenty-five pounds, easy. We were passing garden implements on the wall, pruning shears, trowel, hand pruner, and when he glanced at these, I said, "Please, sir, don't consider that. I know you're a powerful man in this community, but I'm a younger man. With a gun."

His voice was soft, and maybe had some fear in it. "Why don't you just kill me here and be done with it?"

"I'm not here to kill you," I lied. "I'm here for an exchange of information."

"About my granddaughter's death?" This had a sharp-edged sound, with no fear, as he glanced tight-eyed over his shoulder.

"Assuming she's dead, yes," I said.

We were just moving into the kitchen, past cupboards and a refrigerator and stove that were all out of date for such a wealthy homeowner. A pan of tomato soup simmered on the stove, its comforting smell in the air. I glanced right at the big, many-paned window, with its filmy curtains tied back, which had provided such a generous view of his soup-eating.

I said, "I don't want to talk in here. Let's go in your study."

He had his hands up, though I hadn't told him to. "Did Vale hire you? Did that son of a bitch—"

"You're reading it wrong," I said, though he really wasn't far off. "You lead the way."

But he didn't move.

Sneering back at me, he said, "Don't you know the layout of the house? Haven't you done your homework?"

"You were afraid before. Not a bad idea to stay that way."

"I'm going to be eighty in a few months. How afraid of death do you think an eighty-year-old man can be?"

"Judging by my experience? Pretty fucking afraid. Let's *go*. I don't want to stand here with a gun in my hand in a bright room by a window."

He led me to a hallway, where at my bidding he switched on the light. I didn't want to be walked through a dark house by its owner. This was clearly a dangerous man. Just as he needed not to underestimate me, I needed to pay him the same respect.

Passing archways, I got glimpses of a very femininely decorated home in the French Provincial Style. This was still his late wife's house. Whether he'd left it that way out of love or respect, I couldn't say. I doubted it was laziness.

The room he led me to—the addition on the far side of the house—was as much den as study, a deep narrow space with a brick fireplace facing you upon entering. Over it was a big gold-framed oil painting of the Mr. and Mrs. Clarence Stockwell of thirty or forty years ago—the powerful banker and his trophy wife, a beautiful blonde combination of daughter Jenny and granddaughter Candy…and indeed the source of those green translucent eyes.

Yet despite the dead woman's looming presence, this was a man's room—dark wood paneling, Oriental carpet, to the right a pair of comfy brown-leather recliners facing a console TV with a big 25" tube, to the left an office area dominated by a massive mahogany desk surrounded by built-in bookcases extending above and below and around windows. A comfortable-looking tufted leather visitor's chair was positioned opposite.

This was where Clarence lived—here and the kitchen and a bedroom upstairs, probably. The rest of the house belonged to his late wife.

"You take that," I said, pointing to the tufted leather guest chair, and got back behind the desk, settling myself into the swivel number. A drawer back there might have a gun in it, and I didn't want this getting ugly.

He complied, sitting arrow-straight, as if in defiance, his hands on his knees, his chin up. In his tie and white shirt and suit pants, he looked like an over-the-hill waiter about to get a dressing-down.

"Relax," I said. I wasn't pointing the nine millimeter at him, my elbow propped against an armrest, the weapon firmly but casually in hand.

"I'm fine," he said.

"No. You're making me nervous. Relax."

He let air out, a lot of it. He crossed his legs. Folded his arms. Some of the stiffness went away.

"Good," I said. "Do you smoke?"

"No. Why, do you?"

"No, that shit's bad for you. Not smoking must've helped you make almost eighty. I just thought it might put you at ease."

His face clenched in a fist-tight frown. "Let's just get this over with, whatever the hell it is."

"All right. I'm an interloper. The details aren't important, but I knew who those two men were, and why they were in Stockwell, and I stopped them."

He narrowed his eyes as he picked his words with painful care. "The two men. The…two men carrying out the assignment…?"

"I'm not wearing a wire, and if I were, this would be way past entrapment, Mr. Stockwell. You can talk freely. Call them assassins, hitmen, contract killers, whatever you're comfortable with."

"A rose by any other name," he said dryly.

"Right. I stopped them."

His chin raised just a little, but not a defensive gesture. "Meaning you…killed them?"

"Like you said—by any other name. I'm not going to provide

any details. I'll say this much—one handled surveillance on Vale, the other was here to do the killing. Did you know that was how it worked?"

He shook his head.

"You didn't hire them directly?"

He shook his head again.

"You approached a middleman, by networking through a mob source...some Chicago connection...dating back to your dog track days."

His eyes widened briefly and again his chin lifted. This was only the second time I'd really surprised him tonight. "Who *are* you, Mr. Quarry?"

"I told you. An interloper. So the middleman hasn't called you, today, yesterday? To inform you of the death of one or more of the men he sent?"

"No."

"You were not aware that this thing had started to go south?"

"Absolutely not."

I believed him.

"Okay, Mr. Stockwell. You almost certainly will be hearing from the individual you dealt with. You may be told that the contract is kaput, or you may be told a replacement team will be sent. I really have no idea which. You might be asked to put up more money, and you would have every right to refuse. You might suspect you're being taken advantage of, and I would tend to agree, because why would you pay more just because *his* people screwed up?"

"Who the hell are you?"

"Not a reporter. But I *have* been doing some digging. And here's what I don't understand. Here's why you are still alive."

He tasted his tongue. "You have my attention."

"Whatever minor association you had, decades ago, with the

Chicago Outfit, you are not a criminal. You were born into a
wealthy family, a family that had to make adjustments when
their wealth-creating business went bust. So you learned to
be a businessman, and a damn good one. Were you in the
military?"

"No."

"Doing the math, I figure you were probably too young for
the First World War, too old for the second, way too old for
Korea."

His frown mingled irritation and confusion. "Why is that significant?"

"It's significant because you didn't go to war and learn to kill
people. The kind of attitude toward life and death that you can
acquire in war, that's not an apparent part of who you are."

"Why do I have the sense, Mr. Quarry, that it *is* part of who
you are?"

I smiled. "Because you're an astute businessman, Mr. Stockwell. You have dealt with a lot of people of a wide variety in
your long experience. But my point is—you haven't routinely
been involved in criminal enterprises. For one thing, no need.
You own the town."

"That's an exaggeration."

"But not much of one. And, as I say, you are not a killer. Yet
you reached back into your family's one major brush with the
mob to arrange not just a killing, but for someone to be tortured to death. That's extra. Very expensive. And it speaks of a
depth of revenge. Of hate."

His arms were unfolded now, elbows on the armrests. "I
loved my granddaughter very much."

"That part of it, I understand. That I get. That kind of emotion, that's something almost any of us can wrap our head around.
But why are you so sure of yourself in this?"

This frown was strictly confusion. "I don't follow…"

"You wouldn't target Roger Vale for torture and death lightly. And I have to tell you, sir, that I have done some due diligence here. I have investigated, in a limited but experienced way. Your granddaughter may not be dead. She could be a runaway."

"No."

"I understand why you consider it unlikely, but it's possible. Or she could have gone off to a big city and met with an unfortunate end before she had a chance to get in touch with her father, and say she was sorry and please Daddy send me a plane ticket. First class, as your son pointed out. No, she was a beautiful, sexually desirable young woman. She could easily meet with a tragic end on her first night in a big bad city."

"No."

"But if she *was* murdered—and that murder had been made to look like a disappearance—the possible suspects here in Stockwell are many. I *know* you loved your granddaughter, sir, but…she was sexually promiscuous. I think you know that."

He grunted something that was not quite a laugh. "It seems to run in the family."

"Your daughter is another story. I think you probably spoiled her like Candy's father spoiled his daughter. It led to some unfortunate things in both instances, but Jenny is really a good daughter, sir, and you should appreciate her more, what a smart, unique person she is, whatever her quirks. You might want to shift some of that love for your dead granddaughter your alive daughter's way, but hey. That's none of my business."

"No it isn't."

"Candy, for whatever reason, had the sort of low self-esteem that leads a girl to seek approval by giving herself to men. She gave herself to a *lot* of men and boys. And any one of them is a candidate for her murder. Roger Vale is a gay dance instructor, and the notion that he is actually pretending so he can ravage young students, well…it seems absurd on its face. That dumb-ass Pettibone kid is a likelier suspect. So is her married choir director, or Christ knows how many of her discarded sexual partners. *Why* Roger Vale?"

"Because, Mr. Quarry," he said, "he killed her. And…and did God knows *what* else to her before that."

And he began to cry.

Just as his son had, in that insurance office, only harder and longer. He fished a handkerchief from his pocket—he was of an age that still carried those—and covered his face in it, like me covering Farrell's face with a pillow.

When it subsided, he blew his nose, put the hanky away, and said, "Sorry."

"That's okay. Vale. Why are you so sure?"

He was still working at getting his composure back. Then he made a circular gesture with a forefinger toward the desk, and asked: "Could we trade places please?"

I didn't answer right away.

He said, "There's no weapon in any of the drawers. But there's something I want to show you. May I get back there?"

I nodded, rose, and vacated the swivel chair. We swapped places, but I didn't sit immediately, and neither did he. He was reaching for his other pants pocket but froze his fingers before digging into it.

"There's a key I need to get," he said, wanting permission. "I need to unlock a drawer. No weapon, you have my word."

Anyway, like they said in the old cowboy pictures, I still had the drop on him.

"Go ahead," I said.

He nodded thanks, then got out keys on a chain, selected a very small one from among maybe a dozen including house keys, and bent over slightly to unlock a desk drawer to his right. I kept the nine mil trained on him, but what he brought back was a stack of manila file folders, four of them, each around an inch thick.

He sat down and said, "You can look at these at your leisure, Mr. Quarry. I have nothing else planned this evening."

I hadn't reached for them yet. "Maybe you'd care to give me the gist first."

He leaned back in the swivel chair, rocking just a little, like an old man on a sunny porch, but there was nothing sunny about his bleak expression.

"As you may know from Jenny...I would imagine you have utilized her as a source for your inquiries...I hired the National Detective Agency to explore the runaway possibility—they're coast to coast and have the staff and the computer support."

"That's the Pinkertons."

"Yes. But it was a man out of a St. Louis agency who came up with the key piece of information, thanks to a friend on the Missouri state police. Over a period of a year and a half, four teenage girls disappeared who'd made Stockwell Park part of their Spring Break or other vacation plans. None were local— and I've since learned that our mayor made sure it didn't hit the media. Wouldn't want to discourage tourism, after all."

No. Not now that buggy whips were out of fashion. If a Great White had been spotted in that sand-bottomed stream, what was the harm?

"With all those hiking trails," I said, "that park would make a perfect hunting ground for a Ted Bundy."

"That was my exact thinking. I instructed the Pinkertons to look at other disappearances or murders of young girls in parks or other recreational areas. Almost immediately, someone in their western regional office reported that half a dozen girls, over a period of two years, had gone missing in Burton Creek State Park. Vacationers, kids on spring break."

"Sounds familiar."

"All too much so. Burton Creek Park is near Tahoe City, Nevada, so it wasn't certain any one of the girls had disappeared there, just that the park was one of the places they planned to go—and of course Tahoe is more than a 'little' vacationland. These disappearances were over a period of approximately two years, the last Burton Creek incidence just over six years ago."

"And you can connect Vale to those?"

"Decide for yourself, Mr. Quarry. During that same two-year period, in a little town near Tahoe called Incline Village, a Calvin Dorn ran the Dorn Dance Studio. He was very helpful in getting local girls prepared for the Miss Teen Nevada beauty pageant."

"Any pictures of Dorn?"

"He avoided photographers, and when there was publicity in the local press, only pictures of his students appeared. And since it was his own studio, he needed no references, other than materials he self-generated to give to the parents of prospective pupils. He was described as 'discreetly gay' by one Incline Village resident, and there are similar descriptions of him in the Burton Creek folder. Physical description matches Vale, although Dorn was blond and not mustached."

"I'd be less impressed," I said, "if I didn't see those three other folders."

"Yes. Highland Hammocks State Park, four girls disappeared over a year-and-a-half period, near Sebring Florida, where one Corey Ellis ran his Ellis Dance Studio. Then there's Sparta, Wisconsin. The Elroy-Sparta Bike Trail, Buckhorn State Park, Wildcat Mountain State Park, all are near Sparta, where Louis Dane ran the Dane Dance Studio for just under two years.

Helping local girls interested in beauty pageants. Beloved by the parents, and a safely gay man to be working alone with young girls. A total of five girls missing from those state parks. Never local."

"Candy was local."

"There was one other local victim. Heather Foster, sixteen. Hillsboro, Ohio, near Rocky Fork State Park. Heather's body had been dumped in the lake, but it washed up onto the shore—there are before-and-after pictures in the Rocky Fork file. She was a cheerleader, a very popular girl at the local high school. She had been raped, vaginally and anally. Her hands and feet showed signs of severe restraint. Cigarette burns. Small cuts. Finally, death by strangulation—bruising indicated the hands were a male's, not a terribly big male, either."

"Jesus," I said, and I wasn't even looking in the file yet.

"Perhaps the foulest thing of all is…the murdered girl was thought by the other parents of girls to be one that dance instructor Rick Varney had singled out. She'd been his favorite, became his assistant, really his protégée."

Like Sally Meadows.

I said, "No pictures of him?"

He dug into one of the folders. "That's all we have—taken after a recital. This is not the Varney persona, it's the first one we know of—Calvin Dorn."

Dorn was in the background, smiling as he talked to a proud mom, whose arm was around her pretty junior-high-age girl, who was in a tutu and looking adoringly at her dance instructor. The central figure in the photo, an older girl posing, was sharp, as in-focus as the background was blurry. And Dorn had blond hair and no mustache.

But that was Vale, all right, right down to the black tights, black t-shirt and Capezios.

"In every instance, the town was small but not tiny," he said, "maybe ten thousand population, near a vacation area. In every instance, after around two years, he closed down his business pleading financial failure and moved quietly on."

So Candy's diary entries had almost certainly been legit.

"Take your time with those," he said, nodding to the folders.

I gave them a gentle shove back toward him. "No. I believe you. Vale's a serial killer. That's what they call them, you know, the FBI. And that's who this information should go to."

He shrugged. "I discussed that with the Pinkerton people. They say all this is compelling but extremely circumstantial. Further investigation, if I wanted to fund it, might make a difference, and they will be glad to go to the FBI...when the time was right."

"Which file is the one with the photo of the dead girl?"

He pushed it over to me. It was right inside on top, actually both pictures were: a junior high school yearbook-type photo of a beautiful blue-eyed freckle-faced redheaded girl. In the other photo, she was just so much human refuse on a muddy, rocky lake shore.

"Okay," I said. "I get it. This could be what Candy went through. So you wanted him tortured. I can dig it. And what about the girl's father?"

"My son? What about him?"

"Was he with you in this?"

His head rocked back. "Lawrence? Heavens no. He has no stomach for hard decisions. He may have some vague sense that I might be doing something about Vale that, well, steps over the line. But that's all."

We sat in silence for a while.

Then he said, "What now, Mr. Quarry?"

"Why don't you make a phone call?"

"A phone call?"

"Right from your desk here, or from a booth if that's the established procedure. Call whoever set this up for you, and tell him you are cancelling the contract. You understand he's suffered an inconvenience, and intend to pay the full fee. If he mentions that the team he sent to Stockwell has turned up dead, you don't know anything about it. You've just decided to pull the plug."

"*Have* I?"

I sighed. "Understand something, Mr. Stockwell. Nothing against the Pinkertons, but I think you have enough evidence here to easily go to the FBI. You're a powerful man in this state, and no doubt have political strings you can pull. Pull them."

He said nothing. "I could do that. And...actually, the Pinkertons said they would be glad to make the case to the federal authorities for this being a 'serial predator,' in their vernacular. They just preferred to gather more information, but...they *would* do it."

"Not good enough for you, huh?"

"No. Not good enough for me. I wanted him tortured, yes, but not to death...I wanted to know what he'd done to Candy. What he had done with her...her body. Doesn't she deserve a Christian burial?"

"Okay," I said, jumping in fast before he could get emotional again. "And *then* you wanted him tortured to death?"

Stockwell grunted another near laugh. "Yes. I don't believe in hell, and I want him to suffer if not for eternity, for..."

"What seemed like it."

"Yes."

I mulled it a few moments.

Then: "We have a time issue. Vale will be clearing out sooner than later. Obviously, that's his pattern. He stuck around this time because you fingered him to the cops and in the media, and if he ran, it would be an admission of guilt, and he'd have the FBI down on him. He went wrong, picking for a victim a girl from a wealthy, influential family. So he tried to weather the storm, probably planning to pull up stakes in a few months, after the heat died down. Only it never did."

He had been studying me calmly through that. "Vale sent you to kill me, didn't he?"

"Something like that. He thinks I'm killing you right now, and with you dead, he'll figure he has to book it."

"What would you suggest, Mr. Quarry?"

"You're the one behind the big desk. You're the man of means. Why don't you make a suggestion?"

He did: "There's a wall safe behind the portrait of my wife and myself. I can give you ten thousand dollars down, and have another twenty-five thousand in cash for you tomorrow. After it's done. Sufficient?"

I was nodding. "Yeah, generous. But you can afford it. Only… no torture shit. Not even to find out where Candy's body is."

"I could up the ante another ten."

"No. Sorry. Not my scene. But I will gladly remove his evil ass from the planet for you."

He rose, and so did I, and we shook hands.

Then he got me the money.

THIRTEEN

I had a sinking feeling when I pulled into the Vale Dance Studio parking lot around nine-fifteen. I had gone directly there from Clarence Stockwell's, figuring to park on the street till I was sure dance practice was over and all the little girls who studied with this homicidal maniac were safely in the arms of the parents who had entrusted them to him.

But from the front, no sign of lights on within the black bunker gave a first indication that something was wrong.

And when I checked in back, the lot was empty. Not just empty of parental vehicles, but Vale's red Corvette and, for that matter, Sally's baby-blue Mustang.

Nonetheless, I parked near the cement stairs and went quickly up. A neatly hand-lettered sign taped on the inside of the door said

PRACTICE CANCELLED DUE TO ILLNESS.
SEE YOU NEXT WEEK

and signed, "Mr. Roger," with a flourish.

Shit.

He was in the goddamn wind already.

While he figured I was busy ridding him of his Country Club Lane nemesis, Vale appeared to have taken his leave of this latest little town where he helped girls prepare for beauty pageants, among other more overtly perverted pastimes.

With no sign of his vehicle here, maybe he had parked on the street, to discourage any parent from knocking on the door, wanting a better explanation than that note. Or maybe just to wish their beloved Mr. Roger a *Get Well Soon*.

Should I check and see if his Corvette was parked nearby? I decided to skip that; just too unlikely. But was there any chance he might still be in there?

I would have to go inside. Just had to go in and check—what other option was there?

The deadbolt at the double back doors took fifteen seconds to crack with a tension-wrench pick and a short-hook pick, so small they tucked into my billfold. By the way, if that's the kind of lock you're using, just stack your valuables on the porch, so you can get a good night's sleep, undisturbed.

I slipped inside, nine mil in one surgical-gloved hand, moving forward, a lone player on a darkened stage. I stood there listening, like an actor seeking applause, and could hear only my own breathing. It was cold in here. Maybe he'd shut the heat off when he left, like the rich guys turning off lights they didn't need. That prompted a memory of the light switch Vale had used, over on the far wall, which brought up subdued audience lighting. This guided my way through the empty seating back to the little lobby area, whose glowing red EXIT sign helped just enough.

The door to the living quarters at right was unlocked, and I went in low and fast, gun poised; but no one was in there. I almost wished the bastard would jump out at me like Anthony Perkins in *Psycho*, so I could at least have a chance at him. The only sign that he had vacated was the rolltop desk, which had been cleaned out, all the paperwork gone.

Otherwise, everything was here—the furniture, of course— I didn't really think he'd rushed out and rented a U-Haul since I talked to him earlier. The wall hangings, from photos of dance recitals to the framed Broadway posters, were still in place.

Damn things were even hanging straight. The fridge had food in it, including half a six-pack of Diet Coke.

In the wind, all right.

The door to the bedroom across the lobby, a room I'd never been into before (no inclination, really), was also unlocked. I hit the wall switch just inside the door to reveal a chamber with alternating red and black walls, particle-board on the outer ones, the building's natural concrete block walls for the other two. The effect was more bad bowling shirt than Satanic, but knowing who slept here and the kind of fun and games he engaged in did creep me out some.

Particularly since the bed—another goddamn waterbed!— was an oversize round thing with red silk sheets and curving, black-leather-padded headboard. A black dresser stood against a red wall, a red dresser against a black, both secondhand-store jobs repainted.

And each dresser's drawers yawned open and empty. This was not a ransacking but a hasty departure. Closet doors painted black like the rest of a wall opened to reveal empty hangers. A couple of squat but comfortable-looking black leather chairs were angled on a black furry throw rug on the wooden floor, facing a mammoth Sony projection TV, 50" easy, against the other black wall. The big TV was hooked up to a Betamax that sat on a black cabinet perhaps five feet tall and three feet wide, with a little padlock.

A swipe with the butt of the nine mil got rid of the lock, and I swung open cabinet doors that had shelves on their inside, expanding the shelves within—rows and rows of homemade Beta tapes, each spine labeled with dates and names.

Names like Jane, Denise, Cheryl, Suzanne, Jill, Terri, over a dozen names and scores of videotapes, dates as old as eight years back and as recent as last month. How he must have hated to leave this treasure trove of priceless memories behind. Another, even better indication of his haste. No video camera, though. He must have taken that with him.

Or had he?

Above the bed was a ceiling fan with light fixture sporting a cluster of lights. Between bulbs I could spy the circular glass eye of a video camera mounted up there in a black box attached to the black ceiling. From the bed, Vale wouldn't even have to say, "Action." He could just hit the remote. Most of his co-stars probably didn't even know they were in the movies.

I went back over to the cabinet of video cassettes. These were the homemade horrors and delights that Roger Vale relished making and viewing. Underage porn and, in very special instances, do-it-yourself snuff flicks. No need to frequent the XXX section behind the beaded curtain of a video store when you had such a unique collection waiting at home.

Then I noticed something on the floor, not far from the cabinet, apparently tossed there in haste. On first glance, it looked like an iron.

On closer look, I could see that it was a Realistic brand "High Power Audio/Video Eraser."

So he had destroyed the evidence, and done the parents of his victims the one favor he and they could share: with the help of Radio Shack, he had removed the visual record of the degradation suffered by the girls whose names were hand-lettered on the white spines of the now blank videotapes.

But as I quickly checked, several names that might be expected were conspicuous in their absence.

Where was Candy Stockwell among these small-town starlets?

Where was the video record of her death? Nothing on Sally Meadows, either. Or Heather Foster, the Rocky Fork victim whose body had washed up on a lakeshore as evidence far more terrible than any video cassette.

Had he taken with him the most precious tapes? The ones that chronicled his most extreme pleasures, the sex murders of teenage girls? Horrible as that evidence most certainly would be, it *was* evidence, and knowing it had been discovered might— in a unique if unspeakable way—give closure to families with missing daughters.

Those tapes, if they existed, should be found.

And now they were likely with the auteur who'd shot them.

In the wind.

In my Holiday Inn room, I began to pack. Nothing else for me to do here, besides go over to Country Club Lane and wake Clarence from a less than restful sleep, and return his money. That further twenty-five grand he'd promised was a pipe dream now. I'd been too late. We'd both been too late. And now the FBI would have to pick up the ball.

Which meant the sooner I left Missouri's Little Vacationland, the better. Maybe I would stop and say goodbye to Jenny. I sighed and shook my head. Probably not wise.

I sat at the foot of the bed and stared at my suitcase. Was there any other play for me to make here? I could think of none. I'd been beaten, beaten by a goddamn manipulative sociopath, and all I had to show for it was the exhaustion of a long and stressful day. Could I afford to grab a decent night's sleep, and check out in the morning? That way I could stop at Clarence's office at the bank to return his money. And maybe say goodbye to Jenny....

These last-ditch thoughts and hopes had just about congealed into the realization that I needed to get the fuck out of Dodge, *now*, when the phone rang.

I frowned at it.

Clarence Stockwell should know better. What the hell was he thinking, calling me here? I understood that he'd be anxious to know how I'd fared on my mission, but I'd given him strict instructions not to get in touch. *Don't call me, I'll call you.* Fucking businessman of his standing ought to be the fuck familiar with *that* concept.

I answered it anyway.

"Yeah?"

"Jack…oh God, Jack."

It was a female voice.

"…Jack, he's here at my house…"

Whispering.

Frightened.

"…he's crazy, running around…crazy…"

Sally.

"…he says he's leaving and wants to take me with him…I said I didn't want to go, and now…I don't know what the fuck he's going to do, Jack…."

"Honey, just take it easy."

"…I'm afraid, Jack, I'm really, really afrai—"

And the line, as they say, went dead.

The charcoal clouds were rolling again, but no thunder growl or electrical strobe signaled rain, or would that be snow, considering the temp? Would one of those freak snowstorms with lightning erupt to make this night even weirder?

I was guiding the Pinto, no lights, down the gravel road with the walls of cornstalks hovering on either side of me, the breeze catching them, making them rustle, making shivering shapes out of them, as if they too felt the cold.

I could see the farmhouse up ahead, and the barn Sally rented out, and two cars parked where the gravel lane widened—his red Corvette, her blue Mustang. I swung the car over off the gravel onto what little shoulder there was, brushing up against the scratchy stalks, their fingers clawing and scraping at the vehicle.

I got out and crept along the edge of the cornfield, staying low, the nine mil in my right hand, again in surgical gloves. Still in my white shirt and tie, fleece-jacket over them. The .38 snubnose was in my left jacket pocket, the switchblade in my right pants pocket, the hunting knife clipped in its sheath on my belt.

There it was, the moon, gray balls of cloud rolling to either side to give it a window to throw ivory across the rural landscape and, along the way, bathe me in light that I didn't want. I waited for those clouds to roll back over it and conceal the motherfucker, but they didn't.

Moonlight or not, I had to cross the open space between the edge of the cornfield and the two vehicles sitting on that gravel apron.

I took several breaths, my exhales like car exhaust in the chill, then made my move. If I'd been hunkered down any lower, I'd have been crawling. As it was, I moved like an ungainly Munchkin. The moon loved me, stroking me, bringing out my hidden beauty.

Seconds that felt like minutes later, I was behind the Corvette, where I withdrew the hunting knife from its sheath and cut a nice wide gash in a beautiful tire, letting out air that also smoked in the night, hissing like a cranky librarian. I did both rear tires, just to be safe. Then I did the same thing to the rear tires of Sally's Mustang, next to the SALLY vanity plate, figuring she would understand when I explained I did not want to give the man terrorizing her any means of escape.

Quite a few lights were on in the house, both upstairs and down, squares of subdued yellow indicating shades were pulled. The windows were mismatched, as if the builder, likely the farmer himself, had used whatever he could salvage or pick up cheap. A side section looked tacked on, its roof a little crooked. How Mateski would have loved this slapped-together place— one of his ugly paintings come to life.

Now I had to cross the distance between the Corvette and the house. Again, I stayed very low but moved quickly, and then I was at the side of the house.

And heard something—*a muffled cry.*

I knelt by a round-topped many-paned window, just another weird element in the patchwork place, and peered in and, Christ, there she *was...*

...Mustang Sally herself, in a skimpy scarlet nightie, bathed in the stark illumination of a single hanging bulb, heavy coils of hemp rope securing her to a vertical steel post, looped around the post and her wrists—you could hitch a fucking yacht with that much rope. Her red lipsticked mouth filled with an S&M-style ball gag that strapped behind her head, her big blue eyes screaming at me, her long tawny hair a frizzy flowing mane that seemed as hysterical as she was.

I raised a reassuring hand, gave her a look that said, *Stay calm*, and she nodded in frantic understanding.

Then I looked for a way in. The big roundtop window seemed secure. Another more traditional basement window was no help, either. But in back of the house were double storm doors that led down into the basement. They had a simple padlock.

Also back there, up four sloppy wooden steps, was a kitchen door. I went cautiously up and glanced in—the kitchen, looking like it hadn't been remodeled since the '40s and shy of appliances or much of anything really, showed no signs of life. Certainly no sign of Vale. I tried the back door. Locked.

Both my options were fairly easy pickings, literally, but I went with the padlock. That would take me directly down into the basement to get to Sally. We could duck right back out the storm doors and to my car, where I could deposit her while I went back and dealt with this prick.

The same two tools from my billfold that I'd used on the deadbolt at the dance studio worked on the padlock, only in five seconds, not fifteen. My biggest worry was making too much noise lifting one of these ancient wooden-slat doors. I shifted the nine mil to my left hand, then slowly eased open the right-hand door. It creaked, but nothing major.

Soon I had gone down the handful of cement steps into the dirt-floor cellar, letting the door gently back down behind me. Sally was beaming over at me, a sexual sadist's fantasy realized with that ball gag and nightie and heavy rope binding her.

Nine mil still in my left hand, I undid the buckle at the back of the ball gag strap and it fell into her lap.

"Jack," she whispered. "Thank God. You're wonderful."

I whispered back: "Where is he?"

"Upstairs somewhere. Can't you hear him?"

I couldn't. Turning, I looked up the steep steps. "First things first," I said. "Get you untied and out of here, then I can—"

I heard something and swung my gun and myself in that direction—an old furnace and a newer water heater on a little cement platform.

Nothing.

"Those things make noise," I observed, and then I felt something small and metallic and very much like the nose of a revolver in my neck.

"Fooled you!" Sally said giddily. "Toss that gun—not hard, 'cause they go off!"

Shit fuck cunt piss hell, said the bishop when it hurt when he peed.

I said to her, "The ropes—trick knots you could slip right out of?"

"That's right! Roger taught me." Then she yelled: "*Sweetie! Olly olly oxen free!*"

"What are you, six?" I snarled at her—she was still behind me, and, yes, that was a revolver's nose.

"No," she said. "*Twenty*-six."

"I should have known," I said with a dry laugh. "Those posters were the wrong era. Jimi, the Fudge, the Doors…here I thought you just had good taste."

"I *do* have good taste," she said kittenishly. "Didn't I taste good? You tasted good."

The door up there in the kitchen opened and I heard his footsteps on the wooden steps before I saw him. Actually, I saw his gray tennies with white laces first. Then Roger Vale, in a black t-shirt under a Members Only jacket with gray slacks, trotted down into view and came down to stand smiling before me, hands on his hips. No weapon in sight. Putting about four feet between us.

"How'd we do tonight, Quarry?" he said, grinning. He had shaved off the mustache, getting ready for his next role. His hair had a brown tint now. "Did the old man die easy or slow?"

"Not at all," I said. "Alive and well. I finally figured out I was working for the wrong guy."

He frowned. "Well, *that* pisses me off. He's *really* alive, Quarry?"

"That's right."

"Do I get a refund?"

"Oh, did you ask me out here to pay me, Roger? Or to tie off a loose end?"

A sharp laugh; he was already over the disappointment of Clarence being among the living. "And now you're, what? Here to kill me for the old fart?"

"No. I thought you'd be in the wind by now." I did a tiny

head bob back at Sally, whose revolver continued to kiss the back of my neck. "I was just rescuing the damsel in distress."

He chuckled. "She's fantastic, isn't she? You'd never believe she wasn't a teen."

"I'm starting to believe it."

He frowned and grinned simultaneously. "What have you got *on* there, Quarry? Are those surgical gloves? Planning on performing an operation?"

"Maybe."

His expression turned stone serious, as he looked past me to his partner. "You be very careful. Mr. Quarry here is a very dangerous individual…I'm going to get the weapons off him. Be ready to squeeze that trigger, babe."

"You got it," she said.

"Take off your coat," he told me, "slowly, and hand it to me. Nice and easy."

I did, that revolver nose hard against the top of my spine all the way.

He removed the .38 from my jacket pocket, pitched the gun gently to the dirt, sending it a distance. Tossed my jacket to land on top of the nine mil, also a ways away.

I said to the girl with the gun, conversationally, "That was a good story, about your aunt and living by yourself. Any of it true?"

"A long time ago," she said, "some of it was."

"Helpful, Roger," I said, giving him a casual smile, "having a high school girl on the inside, to steer victims your way."

He shook his head and smiled at me as if disappointed. "Oh, it wasn't like that. Mostly we seek out girls who like to party. Who, like the song says, *wanna* have fun. Candy was one of those."

"But the fun got out of hand."

"Sometimes it did," he said, trying to look sad but still smiling.

"With Candy it did. She was a wild thing herself, and it sort of…escalated. We don't do it that often, our…*special* thing. Once or twice, maybe three times a year. All the rest of the girls, well, it's more or less consensual. None have ever ratted us out."

"I think a few *did* rat you out," I said, challenging him gently. "Heather Foster, for example."

That startled him. His head moved to one side, slightly, but he looked at me straight on, eyes tensed. "Where did you hear *that* name?"

"Clarence Stockwell. He has the names and places of all of your unwilling playmates."

His smile was weak. "No. I don't know how you stumbled onto that *one* name, but—"

"What were some of the places? Funny names, some of them. Buckhorn. Rocky Fork. Highland Hammocks. Right, Mr. Dorn? Or is that Dane? No, wait, it's Varney, isn't it?"

He was not happy, a vein standing out on his forehead like a welt. "You shut up! Sweetie, come around and take that hunting knife off of him."

The cold nose of the gun gave me one last kiss and then she stepped around in front of me, an insane little bitch whose pert breasts overflowing the red nightie did not do a fucking thing for me. Even my dick pulled its head in for safety. We were both ashamed of ourselves for banging this little sociopath in her glow-in-the-dark snatch.

She passed Vale her revolver, and was approaching me when he stopped her by the arm. He said to me, "Wait a second, hon. Stand back a tetch. Quarry. Empty your pockets first."

I took my car keys and my Holiday Inn room key from my left pocket and tossed them on the dirt.

"Check it," he told her, and she did, leaning toward me to pat the pocket.

"Nothing," she told him.

She smiled up me, pretty as Charlene Tilton, crazier than a shithouse rat.

Eyes still on me, but speaking to him, she asked, "Can't we have some fun with him first? Does it always have to be girls? He's got a nice motion in his ocean."

I said, "It's just the waterbed."

"You're funny," she said, backing away just a little. "Now the other pocket, honey."

I reached in there and withdrew the switchblade, clicking it open as I did, and swung the blade across her throat, getting a good splash of arterial blood in my face for my trouble, but it couldn't be helped, though I must have looked like a goddamn lunatic. Her amazed gaping face above the gaping wound tilted left and then right, like her head was trying to decide whether to fall off, squirting red along the way, and she was between me and Vale, when he fired, accidentally shooting her in the back of the head, with her own damn gun. I'd already ducked down, not wanting the bullet to find me, and that spatter, at least, missed me, brains and bones and what had been a big blue eye splashing against a cement wall and dripping like a big squashed bug, his shot propelling her forward, the bloody mess of her on top of me now.

He had a little blowback blood on his face, too, though he hardly needed any to look nuts, as he leaned in to try to get a decent shot at me and, with the dead bitch still on top of me, I whipped the thin sharp blade out and down his right wrist, drawing a red line. He yiped, the fingers of that hand popping open, the revolver falling away. I kicked at it, sending it across the room, way back by the furnace.

If I'd been him, I'd have grabbed one of the other guns off the floor and kept at it, but my coat was covering one, the .38 God knew where, Sally's revolver back by the furnace now, and anyway he wasn't used to dealing with people who could really fight back, so he made a scrambling retreat up the stairs, tripping a little, but making it.

I shoved dead Sally off of me, onto her back, then paused—*should I take time to go after one of the guns?* What the hell, I wanted him, and I wanted him right now, and I still had the switchblade in hand. I didn't figure him for having a gun up there, because if that was the case, wouldn't he have brought it down with him?

I was almost to the top of the steps when it occurred to me that there'd be knives in the kitchen....

But when I got to the kitchen, he was already in the dining room, and when I got to the living room, he was halfway up the stairs. He was athletic, dancer that he was. *Was he after something?* Was *there a gun up there?*

I took the steps three at a time, yet when I got up to the hallway, saw no sign of him. Half a dozen rooms up here, including the bath. But as I moved slowly down the hall, I noticed that all the doors stood open but one—the door to that bedroom where Sally had done her black-light hoochie koo.

I gave the fucking door a good, hard kick, in honor of the sloppy farmer-turned-carpenter who had slapped this house together, and it tore off its hinges, slamming to the floor.

But the room, in all its trippy '70s glory, nightstand lamp on, appeared empty. You can't hide under a waterbed. Maybe he'd ducked into one of those mirrored closets—maybe there was a goddamn weapon of some kind in there....

Contemplating this for half a second, I was still standing on the door when he jumped me from behind, with enough force to knock me down, onto the fallen wood slab, the switchblade flinging itself from my fingers like it was abandoning ship. He had a knee in my lower back, which I'd wrenched in the scuffle with the Pettibone kid, and suddenly my hurt ribs were howling, and he looped an arm around my throat, choking me from behind, yanking my head back, working at breaking my neck. I slipped my hand under myself and with minimal fumbling got the hunting knife from its sheath and with the thing clutched blade-down in my fist, brought it back and down and stabbed and sank it three inches into his right thigh, then yanked it back out, with a little blurp of blood.

He screamed and reflexively relaxed his grip on my neck, and I bucked, threw him off, and got to my feet, only to find him sprawled on his back on the waterbed, trying to get his balance, like a bug on its shell wiggling its many little legs.

I climbed onto him like I wanted to fuck him, but in case he was getting the wrong impression, I pressed a knee into his stomach. His mouth popped open like a fish begging for water.

Which was an excellent goddamn idea.

I lifted the hunting knife high, its wide, sharp blade winking at the wide-eyed man under me, and his eyes were filled with terror, thinking I intended the blade for him; but instead I plunged it down, through the silk sheet, and into the bed. Water gurgled as I ripped open a foot-wide gash.

Then I tossed the knife aside and shoved him through the slit and down under there, held him down with my hands on his neck, while he thrashed and got water everywhere, all over me, my sleeves drenched, but then I had all that blood from Sally on me, so I could stand cleaning up some. He kicked and slapped at the air but he didn't touch me. Drowning takes a while, but with me also sort of strangling him, three minutes, more or less, did the trick.

When I climbed off, he was halfway down inside the bed, which wasn't emptying itself because the tear was on top, just kind of caving in, its contents sloshing. His gray shoes with the white laces were draped over the edge of the wooden frame-work, much of the rest of him submerged, his body lolling a little, maybe the way that girl Heather had, when she rolled into shore.

I retrieved my knives. Found the bathroom and cleaned up, dried off, as best I could. I went downstairs to gather my coat and guns and things. Her red nightie soiled and rumpled and not at all sexy, Sally was on her back on the dirt floor, staring with the remaining big blue eye at the rough-beamed ceiling, her mouth dismayed, her cut throat grinning, a twenty-six-year-old teenager who would never be sixteen again. Or twenty-seven.

Behind the wheel of the Pinto, halfway down the cornstalk lane, I shook my head.

"Fucking amateurs," I said.

FOURTEEN

I went back to the Holiday Inn and showered and fell naked into bed. You might think I'd have trouble sleeping, after that horror show, but you'd be wrong. I was drained of every ounce of energy and emotion, and the idea of getting on the road that very minute was out of the question.

I slept till the seven A.M. wake-up call. Showered again and so on. Some of my clothing from last night was crunchy with dried blood and would have to be tossed rather than cleaned. I found a plastic dry-cleaning bag in the closet and put the things in that, and stuffed it in my suitcase, to dispose of later. My fleece-lined jacket hadn't got any blood on it, which was a relief.

At eight-thirty, I drove downtown to the bank building, three modern stories of brown brick and glass with a little plaza in front and a big parking lot at the rear. I sat in the Pinto and thought things over, waiting for Clarence Stockwell to arrive in his big Lincoln, which he did just before nine. I fell in with him as he walked from the car toward the bank's rear entrance.

"It's done," I said.

"Jesus! You startled me, man."

"He had an accomplice. A woman in her twenties pretending to be a teenager. Enrolled at the high school."

We paused and stepped to one side of glass doors, where other employees were entering, and a few customers, too.

"Come up to my office," he said quietly. "I want the details."

"No. I'm warning you, it got a little out of hand. They're both dead, and I had to do some improvising."

"Improvising...?"

"Can you get my money, right now?"

He nodded without hesitation. "I have cash in a safe deposit box. Why don't you come in?"

"No. Wrap it up in something unofficial-looking and deliver it to me after lunch."

"Where will you be?"

I told him.

Hair ponytailed back, in blue-and-green plaid shirt, acid-washed jeans, and bare feet, Jenny had met me warmly, unannounced at her door at nine-something. Now we were sitting in her kitchen watching as it started to snow a little, just a dusting on the fat pines and skeletal trees of the wooded backdrop playing postcard out the breakfast-nook window. We were both having coffee, after eggs, potatoes and muffins again.

"You have to go?" she asked. "You can't stay for a few days, and just...chill out?"

I was in sweatshirt and jeans. "No. It was messy last night. I don't know where it might lead. And when you see the paper, you may not be so anxious to have me around."

She was a great woman, but the initial official reaction when the two bodies were discovered would be that some crazed murderer had "slain" a dance instructor and a local teenage girl. As opposed to a guy just dealing with what came at him.

Those green translucent eyes in the pretty, sharp-featured face—no makeup at all this morning, and yet pretty as hell—searched me with an earnestness on the edge of tears. I had admitted to her only that I was not a reporter, but an investigator, working for her father.

"When things clear over," she said, "you'll be back?"

"Maybe," I lied. "You need to talk to your old man about this. I'm leaving it up to him, what exactly you know, and how much."

"Can you spend the morning, anyway? When did you say Daddy's coming over?"

"Around one."

"Then why don't we go upstairs and say goodbye?"

We did.

When her father arrived to give me the packet of money, I met him at her front door and said, "Go in and tell your daughter whatever you want to," and left.

I don't know what kind of local coverage it got, but the bizarre "Grand Guignol" crime scene at that slapped-together farmhouse received limited national play for about a week. Then, in a few months or so, the onslaught began.

Five bodies of teenage girls were dug up in that dirt cellar where Sally had played captive, among them Candy Stockwell. The papers did not detail whatever indignities the local girl had suffered before her murder.

Two dozen Betamax cassettes were found in one of four packed bags in the farmhouse. Contents of the tapes were never disclosed to the public, other than a brief statement from the Missouri state police that "the homemade videos confirm Roger Vale and Sally Meadows as accomplices in murder."

Then the FBI got involved.

The back yard of a secluded house outside Incline Village, Nevada, once rented by dance instructor Calvin Dorn, gave up six dead girls.

In Sebring, Florida, a vacant lot adjacent to the one-time Corey Ellis Dance Studio surrendered five dead teenage girls, ages fourteen to sixteen.

A farmhouse outside Sparta, once rented by Louis Dane, yielded a crop of five dead girls.

A cabin rented by Rick Varney, near Rocky Fork State Park in Ohio, offered up three more in its back yard.

Roger Vale was born Louis Peck in Topeka, Kansas, an outstanding high school drama student. Sally Meadows was Lori Reif

of Tahoe City, Nevada, third place runner-up in the 1972 Miss
Teen Nevada pageant—Vale's protégée from the start, nearby
Burton Creek Park raising the curtain on their collaboration.

There would be speculation about what made them tick, the
childhoods that shaped them, and whether mental illness played
a role in the homicidal activities of either or both. To me, they
were just fucking murderers.

Don't forget: there's a difference between a murderer and a
killer. Murderers, like Roger and Sally, lay waste. A killer per-
forms a service.

Sometimes a public service.

I called her, about a year later. Probably should have done it
from a pay phone, but one evening in my A-frame cottage on
Paradise Lake, when nothing good was on TV, and I'd had a few
beers, I impulsively dialed her.

"Jack Quarry," she said warmly. "I'd recognize that voice
anywhere. I hope you're calling to say you're coming back to
Stockwell for a visit."

"Not yet. All that craziness is still unfolding, FBI and CNN.
Some asshole is writing a book."

"Oh, well, it's quieted down here."

"You, uh…after what you must think I did, I'm surprised
you're so…cool about it."

But her voice bore only affection as she said, "You gave my
father his life back. We're almost friendly now, he and I. My
brother is dating a widow almost as wealthy as he is, if you can
imagine."

"Good for them. What about you?"

"Not seeing anybody. Too busy. Speaking of a-holes writing
books, *I've* been writing, really working at it. I've got exciting
news, Jack. I actually finally *sold* a novel, and now I'm on my
second."

"Well, that's great."

"I figured out a handle on this romance thing. To give it a twist of my own. I'm sort of doing westerns but from a female point of view. The new book, the heroine is a schoolmarm who secretly has dark sexual desires."

"Does a stranger ride into town?" I asked.

"Always. My first book was…you'll laugh."

But we already were.

"First book," she was saying, "is about a saloon girl who's the bastard child of the richest rancher in the valley. The second-richest rancher hires a gunslinger, and…well, I hope you'll read it. After all, it's dedicated to you."

"No kidding? What's it called?"

"Don't laugh. *Passion Rides the Prairie*. Come visit and I'll give you a signed copy."

"One of these days."

"You'll probably think it's corny, and I wouldn't blame you. Gary Cooper type drifts into town, cleans up the place, sweeps a frontier gal off her stupid fuckin' feet."

"Why, does that sound so bad?"

"Not at all," she said. "But I guess you only meet heroes like that in books."

Wasn't that the truth?

Want More QUARRY?

Try These Other
Quarry Novels From
MAX ALLAN COLLINS and
HARD CASE CRIME...

The First Quarry

The ruthless hit man's first assignment: kill a philandering professor who has run afoul of some very dangerous men.

Quarry In the Middle

When two rival casino owners covet the same territory, guess who gets caught in the crossfire...

The Last Quarry

Retired killer Quarry gets talked into taking one last contract—but why would anyone want a beautiful librarian dead...?

Quarry's Ex

An easy job: protect the director of a low-budget movie. Until the director's wife turns out to be a woman out of Quarry's past.

More Great Suspense from
HARD CASE CRIME

Two For the Money
by MAX ALLAN COLLINS
AUTHOR OF 'ROAD TO PERDITION'

Master thief Nolan wants to bury the hatchet with the Mob—
but all they want to bury is Nolan.

Dead Street
by MICKEY SPILLANE
PREPARED FOR PUBLICATION BY MAX ALLAN COLLINS

The final novel from all-time bestseller Spillane! Officer Jack
Stang has one last chance to save his girlfriend's life—years
after he thought she'd died!

The Comedy is Finished
by DONALD E. WESTLAKE
THE MWA GRANDMASTER'S GREAT LOST NOVEL

America is finally getting over the nightmares of Watergate and
Vietnam and the national hangover that was the 1960s. But not
everyone is ready to let it go. Not aging comedian Koo Davis,
and not the People's Revolutionary Army, who've decided that
kidnapping Koo could bring their cause back to life...

**Available now at your favorite bookstore.
For more information, visit
www.HardCaseCrime.com**